Vanishing Star

Judy Baer

Cedar River Daydreams

Other Books by Judy Baer

Vanishing Star

Judy Baer

BETHANY HOUSE PUBLISHERS
MINNEAPOLIS, MINNESOTA 55438

All Scripture quotations are taken from *The Everyday Bible, New Century Version*, copyright © 1987, 1988 by Word Publishing, Dallas, Texas 75039.
Used by permission.

The Vanishing Star
Judy Baer

Library of Congress Catalog Card Number 90–56209
ISBN 1–55661–197–8
Copyright © 1991
All Rights Reserved

Published by Bethany House Publishers
A Ministry of Bethany Fellowship, Inc.
6820 Auto Club Road, Minneapolis, Minnesota 55438

Printed in the United States of America

For the people at
Bethany House Publishers
who make it all happen.
Thank you.

"Continue to think about the things that are good and worthy of praise. Think about the things that are true and honorable and right and pure and beautiful and respected."

Philippians 4:8

Chapter One

"I wish someone would turn down that music," Binky McNaughton complained. She glared at the backs of the Hi-Five girls standing at the Hamburger Shack jukebox. "Can't they play something quiet?"

"If they played something quiet, we'd fall asleep," Lexi Leighton pointed out. "I'm exhausted." Todd Winston and Jennifer Golden nodded wearily in agreement. "How about you, Egg? Are you tired?" Lexi asked.

Egg McNaughton wilted into the seat like a boneless rag doll. "Tired? Who, me?" They'd all spent the day cleaning and planting trees on the riverfront, a job harder than any of them had anticipated. His gaze followed the Hi-Five girls—Minda Hannaford, Tressa and Gina Williams—as they made their way back to their booth. "Did you see Minda or any of the Hi-Fives at the river today?" he inquired.

His sister Binky snorted. "What? Lower themselves to do something as demeaning as picking up garbage? That's for peasants like us, not for important people like Minda and the Hi-Fives."

"Give her the benefit of the doubt, Binky. Maybe they had something else to do today."

"What could be more important than saving Cedar River? The most important thing Minda probably did today was to decide which color lipstick went with her sweater."

"Touchy, touchy," Jennifer commented. "Binky's in a grumpy mood."

Binky's shoulders drooped wearily. "I'm tired! We worked hard." Her red hair looked as if a family of birds had attempted to nest in it.

"Why so crabby?" Todd asked. "Think of the good things that have happened in the past few weeks. I'm planning to spend lots of time down by the river this summer. Now we can play Frisbee, have picnics, go jogging on the paths. Besides that, the people in Cedar River have become more aware of the importance of caring for the environment, thanks to the good work of Egg McNaughton."

Lexi noticed that Minda Hannaford and her friends were eavesdropping intently on their conversation. Although Minda acted as though she wanted nothing to do with Lexi or her friends, she was always curious about what the gang was up to. Lexi had a hunch that Minda, for all her bravado, was jealous of the close friendship that Lexi and the rest of the gang shared. Lexi wished for the day when she and Minda could be friends instead of what they were now—courteous enemies. Lexi's attention was drawn back to the conversation at her table when Binky gave a little squeak of pleasure.

"What did you say?" Lexi asked.

"We've decided to celebrate the end of the Cedar River project. I think we should have a party, don't you?" Binky was off and running. "We should have pizza. Maybe we could churn ice cream or pull taffy. And we need music. Lots of music."

Todd burst into laughter.

"What's so funny?" Binky said indignantly. "I think it's a great idea."

"Just a minute ago you were complaining about the music!" Todd teased with a smile.

"I don't mind celebrating," Egg said wearily, "but I'm not in the mood for doing any work. Pulling taffy and churning ice cream are work."

"Lazy," Binky accused.

"Crazy!" Egg shot back. "We're tired, Binky. You even admitted to that a minute ago." He glanced around the table. They all looked exhausted. "I've got an idea. Let's go to a movie."

"Who celebrates by going to a movie?" Binky wrinkled her nose. "That's boring."

"I don't care. The idea of sitting in a dark theater and having someone else entertain me sounds great. There are a bunch of good ones showing at the Multiplex Cinema. I read the marquee on the way over to the river."

Binky's lower lip protruded for a moment, then a grin broke across her features. "That's right! I remember now. *Chainsaw Slaughter* was showing at one of the theaters. I wouldn't mind seeing that one."

"Ugh!" Jennifer yelped. "That sounds horrible."

"Then how about *Back from the Crypt* or *Dead Man's Shuffle*?"

"Are you sure there isn't something better than either of those?"

Binky wrinkled her nose. "Oh, just some dumb stuff. An animated cartoon for kids, and a couple of mushy love stories. Who'd want to watch any of those when they could see *Chainsaw Slaughter*?"

"I'd certainly prefer them to the horror movies," Lexi said. "They sound too gruesome for me."

"Binky's been on a real horror-movie kick lately," Egg said. "She even videotapes the late-night TV ones so she can watch them after school."

Binky didn't deny it. "Hey, I like them. What can I say? They're fun."

"That's not what I call fun," Lexi murmured.

"Just try it," Binky insisted. "If you don't like it, we can leave. I know where there's a great movie. *Terror Stalks the City* is showing at the Odeon downtown. It's one I've really been wanting to see. Besides, it's probably not as gory as some of the others that are out on video."

"Well, that's good to hear," Jennifer said sarcastically.

"You mean you actually rent those things?" Todd asked, curious.

"You bet. I like to watch them at night after everyone else has gone to bed. I sit in the family room and shake, I'm so scared."

"Boy, that sounds like a lot of fun to me," Jennifer muttered.

Binky cast her a hurt look. "You're laughing at me because I rent horror movies. Well, I'm not the only one, you know. I have to race to the video store when a scary movie comes out on tape. Otherwise there's a waiting list ahead of me."

"You mean normal people are waiting to rent them?" Todd asked. "Or weird people?"

"Not exactly normal," Binky admitted. "I'm always competing with the Hi-Fives for the latest horror movies."

"Really?" Lexi was shocked. She hadn't realized the Hi-Fives were into horror movies.

"It figures," Egg muttered.

Binky poked him in the side with her elbow. "Be quiet, Egg. You don't know how much fun it is to watch horror movies. It's fun to be scared." Her face was animated. "It's exciting to sit in the dark, to have all your nerve endings tingling and to wonder what you'll be screaming at next. It's great when someone with an axe pops out of a closet or a creepy seaweed-covered hand slips over the side of a boat as the hero rows back to shore." Binky was practically trembling. "The gory scenes are interesting because you can analyze the trick photography. I definitely like the bloody ones the best."

"I find this so hard to believe about you, Binky," Todd stared at her in amazement.

"It's fun, Todd. Some people go to movies so they can cry. I like to scream. What's so strange about that? Well, are we going to the movie or not?" Binky demanded. She was the only one of the group that seemed enthusiastic about a movie that involved more knives and blood than a slaughterhouse.

"Just for me? Try it, please?" Binky pleaded. "We can hold hands if we get scared. It's okay to scream as loud as you want in a horror movie. *Terror Stalks the City* is supposed to be really great."

"I can't believe you'd waste your money on that trash," Jennifer said bluntly. "Those horror movies are stupid. You can't even keep the cast straight because they're getting killed off so fast."

"You can criticize me all you want, but there are lots of people in this town that love horror movies. Especially Minda and Tressa."

"Is that supposed to make us interested?" Jennifer muttered.

"There's more to it than the movie. We can buy huge cartons of buttered popcorn and oversized sodas! We'll sit near the front so we can catch every detail. When it gets really gory we can close our eyes and scream our heads off."

"Binky McNaughton, what are we going to do with you?" Lexi said, shaking her head.

Binky grinned impishly. "I wouldn't want those awful things to happen to me or any of us in real life, but when it's all make-believe, it's just fun to get scared."

"Have you had your sister's head examined lately?" Jennifer asked Egg.

"Why?" Egg shrugged. "There's nothing up there to examine. As far as I know, it's completely empty."

Binky eyed her brother with disgust.

"I'm not crazy about horror movies," Lexi offered, "but I suppose I could give it a try. Maybe they've improved."

"No, they're just as bad as ever," Egg assured her.

"How can you say that?" Binky spouted. "You haven't seen *Terror Stalks the City*. I'm sure it's going to be excellent. Loosen up you guys." Binky pushed away from the table. "You'll all love it. Let's go!"

Lexi waited for Todd at the door while Jennifer, Egg and Binky all headed for Todd's '49 Ford Coupe.

"What have we gotten ourselves into?" she whispered to him.

"We're always asking ourselves that—where Egg and Binky are concerned. Frankly, I'd rather see a Western or a comedy, but we can go along with Binky this once. Every horror movie I've ever seen is so fake it's almost funny."

"I guess it's the least we can do for a friend," Lexi agreed.

"Should be interesting." Todd tucked Lexi's hand in the crook of his elbow and they strolled toward the car.

Binky was already in the backseat jumping up and down like a child. "Come on, come on! If we don't hurry, we'll be late, and miss the best seats."

"I haven't seen her this excited since Christmas," Egg said grimly.

"Come on, Egg," Jennifer interrupted. "She's always this excited. Settle down, Binky. We're on our way."

The Odeon was a large, old theater in downtown Cedar River, and was the site of stage productions and concerts as well. It was an ornate structure inside and out with scrolls, columns, and chubby little cupids. The stage was covered with rich burgundy velvet curtains.

"It's really neat in here," Jennifer said, glancing around. "I usually go to the movies at the mall. I'd forgotten how nice this old theater is."

"My family has season tickets for the theater." Todd dug his hand into the box of popcorn he'd bought in the lobby. "We come here once a month to see a play."

"What's this about stage plays?" Binky said, making a face. "You guys are acting so 'high-brow.'"

"We're trying to expose you to a little culture, Binky," Todd teased. "Isn't that OK?"

"Give me a movie that makes your heart jump into your throat. That's what I like."

"Binky, this is a side of you I've never seen," Lexi said. "I always thought you were meek and mild-mannered."

"I am. That's why I like these movies so well. I get all the hostile feelings out of my system without hurting anyone. Isn't that smart?"

Egg made a disgusting noise at the back of his throat. "You could crush soda cans for recycling. Stomp, stomp, stomp. That would get some hostility out of your system."

"Well, I wouldn't have any hostility *in* my system if it weren't for you, Egg."

Before Binky and Egg could get into another one of their typical arguments, Lexi said, "The theater is full already. Do you see five places together?"

Egg craned his neck and gazed around the large auditorium. His arms were filled with boxes of popcorn, red licorice, and quart-sized containers of soft drinks. "Everyone in town must be . . ." His voice caught in his throat as he saw Minda Hannaford, Tressa and Gina Williams sitting near the front of the theater. Egg had had a crush on Minda for months and the sight of her always made him flush a little.

Binky grabbed a box of popcorn and a package of licorice from her brother's hands. "I want to sit down front. I like to be close to the screen so I don't miss anything."

"Wouldn't it be more comfortable toward the back?" Todd wondered, looking at the huge screen.

"You miss the atmosphere back there, Todd. You can't get scared sitting in the back."

"Sorry. You can tell I don't do this often."

"I can see that." Binky shook her head woefully. "You have so much to learn." They trooped toward the front of the theater and squeezed into the same row in which Minda and her friends were sitting.

"Excuse me. Excuse me. Excuse me," Binky chanted as she led the way over the tangle of legs between her and the empty seats. "We're just in time. They're about to turn the lights down." She plopped into a seat with a satisfied sigh, ripped the top off the licorice package with her teeth, wedged the popcorn box between her legs and leaned back. "Ahhh, perfect," she said. "Let the movie begin."

As if on cue, the lights dimmed and the screen blazoned to life. Lexi dug into Todd's large box of popcorn as they watched the movie previews—two upcoming action adventures and one comedy. Lexi's family went to an occasional movie, but she was not like most of her friends who saw every new movie that came out. She couldn't remember the name of the last scary movie she'd been to, but she knew she hadn't liked it. She sighed and sank deeper into the seat, curious to see what it was that fascinated Binky so much. It didn't take Lexi long to realize that whatever intrigued Binky was *not* going to interest her.

The heavy, pulsating music that signaled imminent violence stung her ears. Every time the murderer stalking innocent victims on the streets of New York lunged from behind a garbage can, waving a large knife, or from the dark steps of a fire escape, Lexi closed her eyes. Binky's delighted screeches and squeals were getting on her nerves. In the middle of a particularly gory scene, Lexi covered her eyes.

Todd's voice near her ear made her jump. "They used enough fake blood here to fill a river bed," he whispered.

Lexi peeked at him from beneath her fingers. "Keep reminding me. This is too much for me."

"Look at Binky." Todd gave her a nudge.

Lexi peered around Egg so she could see her friend. Binky was leaning forward in rapt attention, staring up at the movie screen. Her hand moved mechanically from the popcorn container to her mouth. She chewed intently, entranced by the constant action on the screen.

"It's like she's hypnotized!" Lexi whispered.

"I know. Crazy, isn't it? It's as though she's . . . addicted to these things."

Jennifer, on the other side of Todd, was reacting in similar fashion to Lexi. Scrunched down in her seat, Jennifer's hands were poised in mid-air, ready to cover her eyes at the next gruesome scene.

A particularly loud and violent scream cut through the air. Lexi gasped. "We're too close. It's like I'm right in the middle of the action. I don't like it."

Calmly Todd slipped an arm around her shoulders and gave her a squeeze. "It's only a movie, Lexi. Remember that."

"But there're so many people getting hurt, and they aren't catching the killer."

"Only forty-five minutes to go. He'll be caught by then. Just wait and see."

The music reached a crescendo and the violence started again. Lexi closed her eyes and kneaded the tight muscles at the back of her neck. She could hear Binky's delighted squeals with every movement on the screen.

"Come on, get him. Get him! Can't you see who did it? Get him!" Binky was sitting straight up in her chair, beating her small fist against her knee, totally engrossed in the wild tale. "He's right behind you! If you don't turn around, you're going to get stabbed . . . ooohhh. You asked for that, buddy." Binky's eyes reflected the flickering colors on the screen.

Egg muttered into Lexi's ear, "I forgot to mention that Binky really freaks out at these movies."

"I see that."

"Sometimes she's worse." Egg stuffed an entire licorice strip into his mouth. "She's not going to sleep tonight without bad dreams. We can count on that."

In a shocking surprise development on the screen, the masked villain who had just been riddled with bullets, suddenly lunged for the hero in a final desperate attempt at revenge, a death rattle gurgling in his throat. The totally unexpected turn of events sent Binky straight off her seat and onto Egg's lap.

Egg gave a disgusted snort, stood up and dumped his sister back into her seat. "Grow up, Binky! It's just a movie."

At the far end of the row, Lexi could hear Minda and her friends screaming at the top of their lungs. When the movie finally ended and the credits began to roll, Lexi felt limp. She leaned back in her chair and exhaled, "Whew! Am I glad that's over!"

"Me too," sighed Jennifer, "that was disgusting!"

Minda and her friends were still squealing and hanging on to each other. Others in the theater were either laughing or animatedly discussing the movie. They all seemed to love the violence and gore that made Lexi so terribly uncomfortable.

Was she the only one who didn't think these movies were worth watching?

Egg poked Lexi in the ribs. "Look at this, will you?" he said. "And this is her idea of fun!"

Binky was scrunched down in her seat, her eyes squeezed tightly shut, and her face contorted in a grimace. "Is it over? Is it over?" she repeated.

"Yes, it's over, Binky. You can get up now." Jennifer pulled on one elbow while Egg pulled on the other.

"Wasn't it great?" Binky bubbled, her eyes sparkling. "What did you think, Todd? Lexi? Jennifer? Exciting, huh?"

"I don't get it, Binky. Why would you want to see something that scares you so much that we practically have to unglue you from your seat when the movie's over?" Todd asked.

"Well, it wasn't that bad," Binky said. "I just got a little overexcited at the end."

"Overexcited? I think you popped my eardrums," Egg said, sticking his fingers in his ears.

"That's the fun part. I loved it. I wonder if it would seem as scary if I saw it again?"

"You'd pay money to see that again?"

"Sure. It's just like going on a roller coaster ride. You can have all the thrills you want in a nice safe place and you know you can get off at the end. Perfect, don't you think?"

Lexi wasn't ready to agree with that. She had to think about this for a while. What was it about horror movies that made them so popular? What made Binky come back for more?

Chapter Two

As they were expelled onto the street by the flowing crowd leaving the theater, Binky exclaimed, "Ooooh, wasn't that great? My knees are still shaking."

"Maybe we should go to the Hamburger Shack and revive you with a plate of fries," Todd teased.

"Food? After all that gore?" Binky looked like she was going to be sick.

"Maybe fries, but no catsup." She clutched at her stomach. "For a minute there I thought I was going to throw up," she admitted. "Maybe some food would be good."

"She's a mess, Lexi," Jennifer whispered as they made their way to Todd's car. "Why does she do this to herself? It was just a stupid movie."

"You know how Binky is," Lexi said. "She gets so involved in things."

Ahead of them, Binky announced, "I hear there's going to be a sequel. I can hardly wait."

"The girl is a wacko," Jennifer said flatly. "I like a good scary movie once in a while, but this is ridiculous."

Lexi was silent all the way to the Hamburger

Shack. Binky, wound tight as a spring, chattered continuously about the movie. "What did you think when that body fell off the roof? Ooooh, what a shock! And did you see how it bounced off the wall and splattered all over the place? What cinematography!"

"Binky, Todd and I could have done the same thing with a simple video camera!" Egg told her. "Everyone except you could see that it was only a dummy falling."

"You think you're so smart, Egg, but you don't know everything. I'll bet it was a stunt man. Don't you think so, Jennifer?"

Jennifer declined an answer. Binky didn't seem to notice. Instead, she chattered happily about how frightened she'd been.

"I didn't think it was so thrilling," Lexi said quietly.

"Looks like the place is filling up fast." Todd parked the car and they all trooped into the Hamburger Shack single file. Fortunately, their special table at the back was still open. They'd barely settled down when Minda, Tressa and Gina came marching in to claim the booth next to theirs.

"How did you like the movie, Minda?" Binky asked, her eyes bright.

"Dumb, as usual. Not even the least bit scary. I think I fell asleep," Minda said coolly.

Binky's eyes widened. "Really?"

"I can't imagine *anyone* being scared in that movie," Tressa added. She looked slyly at Binky. "Only a child would be scared in a movie like that one."

Lexi could see Binky deflating. Minda and her friends were obviously saying those things just to torment Binky. Fortunately, Jerry Randall came to take their order. The Hi-Fives quickly lost interest in teasing Binky and turned away.

It was Todd who brought up the upcoming tennis tournament. "Have you heard about the big event being sponsored by the local Tennis Association? There's going to be a professional tennis tournament held right here in Cedar River. My tennis coach has been on the committee working to bring it to town. They've been planning this for over two years. Now it's finally going to happen."

"You mean there will be famous people here?"

"There'll be a few—famous in tennis, anyway."

"Those people are almost like movie stars," Binky exclaimed. "Do you think we can get their autographs? Isn't it exciting?"

"Maybe *too* exciting," Egg said moodily. His face was long and his expression sour. "I wonder if Cedar River can stand anymore excitement for a while. I don't know if I can."

"Don't worry, Egg," Lexi consoled him. "You're just tired. By tomorrow, you'll be ready for something new. The tennis tournament sounds perfect."

"I feel really good about it," Todd said. "I've played tennis a long time. This is my chance to meet the best people in the business. Coach Barris promised to line me up with a few of the big names to bat a few balls with them. Wouldn't that be great? The coach asked me to work during the tournament. I said sure, because I'd like to rub shoulders with some of these people." Todd looked sheepishly at Lexi, "I told them you'd work, too, Lexi. Is that all right?"

"That's great! I love to watch tennis. It's my dream to go to Wimbledon."

"I thought so." Todd looked around the table. "Is there anyone else who'd like to be a 'go-fer' for a few days?" he asked. "There's not much to the job. We just have to hang around and be available to run errands for any one of the participants who needs something."

"You mean we might get to meet the celebrities?" Binky was already starstruck. "*I'll* do it."

"Me too," Egg chimed.

"Me three," Jennifer added with a grin.

"The pay isn't much and the hours are long, but it'll be a lot of fun."

"How many people do they need, Todd?" Jennifer asked. "Maybe Peggy Madison would like to help out, too."

"Peggy's going to visit her grandmother. She won't be around for a few weeks," Lexi informed her.

"That's too bad," Jennifer said. "It would have been good for her. She's more shy and quiet than she used to be."

Lexi didn't comment. She had kept Peggy Madison's secret that she had left Cedar River the year before to have a baby. Lexi also knew that returning to Cedar River and pretending that her life had not changed was very hard for Peggy.

"I'll tell her about it," Lexi said, "but I'm sure she won't be able to do it."

"That's really unfortunate," Todd added. "Because Peggy's an athlete, I'm sure she'd enjoy meeting Holly Agnew."

"Holly Agnew! *The* Holly Agnew? The famous teenage superstar? I just read about her in the newspaper yesterday!" Binky practically floated from her seat. "She's one of the best female tennis players in the world today, and she's our age!"

"She's the biggest star taking part in the tournament," Todd confirmed. "I saw the promotional material the committee's using. Holly's name is splashed all over everything. They consider her a real drawing card. Even people who don't normally like tennis will watch someone like Holly."

"I am *so* excited," Binky squealed. She clapped her hands and bounced on the seat. "I'm going to meet Holly Agnew! Tell me all about her, Todd."

"You probably know as much about her as I do, Binky. She's in all the newspapers and news magazines. They call her the 'Teen Tennis Queen.' She started playing when she was very young. Coach Barris says she has the potential to be the biggest and best tennis star America's ever had if she keeps playing the same powerful game she has till now. Holly has already earned more money than most people earn in a lifetime. Coach Barris got a letter from her agent mentioning that she'd just signed contracts to endorse tennis clothing and a soft drink. If she never played another game of tennis she'd still be a millionaire."

Binky's eyes were wide with excitement. "A millionaire at sixteen? I can't believe it."

"From what I've read, she's earned it," Jennifer commented. "She's got an excellent serve."

"And a super backhand," Lexi added. "Besides that, she's fun to watch on the court."

"She's pretty tall. That's all I know about her," Egg said.

"Five foot seven and a half," Todd added. "That's where her strength comes from. She has terrific concentration when she's playing a match. Nothing fazes her. I hope I can learn something from her while she's here."

"Imagine. Holly Agnew here in Cedar River." Binky slouched against her seat, her eyes glazed with wonder.

"You're not going to act like some kind of a stupid groupie, are you Binky?" Egg asked, concerned. "Even though she's rich and a great tennis player, she *is* just a teenager like us."

"I can't think of anything about her that would be like us, except that she's a teenager," Binky said huffily. "She's beautiful. She's famous. She's rich." Her shoulders drooped dejectedly. "She'll never even look at us. I just know it."

"Aren't you being a little quick to judge this person?" Lexi asked. "You've already decided she'll never speak to any of us. If I were her, I wouldn't appreciate that conclusion."

"Oh, Lexi. You're always so fair. Not everyone in this world is fair, you know. She's probably going to hate us."

"I don't think we can expect too much," Todd said frankly. "She'll be very busy while she's here. The tennis tournament will get a lot of national coverage."

"You mean, we might be on TV?" Egg brightened

immediately. "Do you think someone might inter-view one of us?"

Binky kicked Egg under the table. "What do you have to say that anyone would care to hear?"

"I could tell them about our recycling project," Egg said hopefully. "Maybe I could slip in a little reminder about the environment."

"Oh, Egg. You don't ever give up, do you?" Binky and Egg continued their familiar banter.

Lexi noticed that the Hi-Fives in the next booth had become very quiet. Lexi had a hunch they were listening for more facts about Holly Agnew and the upcoming tennis tournament.

As if to feed their curiosity, Todd repeated, "Well, she's sixteen, like most of us, but she's been playing tennis since she was four, so her life is quite different than ours, to say the least."

"Egg wasn't even walking when he was four," Binky quipped, ducking to avoid the wad of paper Egg tossed at her.

"Holly travels with her coach and a couple of companions," Todd continued. "My coach will rent a house for them, a place Holly's coach picked out. He said he needed a large accommodation so they could all be together. She also travels with a tutor so she won't fall behind in her schoolwork."

"It certainly sounds like a different life than we're used to in Cedar River," Jennifer agreed.

Minda Hannaford, who'd been listening to the conversation, turned around and leaned over the back of the booth. "So what's the big deal?" she asked.

"About Holly Agnew?" Binky fluttered her eyelashes. "If you've been eavesdropping, you had to have heard that she's a famous millionaire at just sixteen years old."

"So what?" Minda shrugged. "She's probably also a spoiled brat. She's got to be if she has a tutor traveling with her wherever she goes. I think the whole thing is boring. I think Holly Agnew is boring and I'm sure that the tennis tournament will be boring too."

"How can you say that, Minda?" Binky was indignant.

"Maybe this town is enough for *small minds*, but for most of us it's a place where nothing's happening." Minda tossed her long blond hair with her hand. "Frankly, I'm beginning to think that the whole town of Cedar River is boring."

"Boring" was obviously Minda's latest complaint. If she disliked the town so much and thought everything was so dull, why didn't she do something about it? Lexi wondered.

"This really has to be the dullest town in the whole country," Tressa Williams chimed in.

"Maybe the whole world. What girls like us need is some action!" Minda proclaimed. "And there's certainly none here."

"Even that dumb town in the movie we just saw where everyone was getting axed and murdered was better than Cedar River." One of the Hi-Fives giggled.

"Yeah, there was nothing boring about that town," someone else agreed.

"Well, if you're so bored, why don't you go bowling?" Binky suggested.

"Bowling? Really, Binky, bowling is for nerds."

"How about racquetball?"

"Oh, no. I don't want to get all sweaty. It ruins my make-up."

"So, take a walk."

"I haven't got the right kind of shoes."

Binky glared over the back of the booth at Minda and her friends. "I don't think it's this town that's boring. I think you girls are boring!"

Minda eyed Binky coldly. "Then you've got another thing coming, Binky McNaughton. I say that what this town needs is to be stirred up a little."

"Right. You bet," the Hi-Fives chimed in agreement.

"What do you mean by stirred up?" Lexi wondered, uncomfortable with the conversation. She didn't like it when Minda was in one of her negative moods.

"Never mind," Minda retorted.

"Yessir," Tressa agreed, "I think this town needs a little excitement."

Minda slid out of her seat. "You mean, this *boring* town needs excitement. Bor-ing. Bor-ing. Bor-ing." The girls sauntered off, chanting the word over and over.

"Now what do you think they meant by all that?" Lexi asked suspiciously.

Todd shook his head and shrugged. "There's no way I can figure them out."

"I think they were just trying to get on your nerves," Jennifer mused. "Especially after they heard how excited everyone is about Holly Agnew coming to town."

Binky gave a little sound of disgust. "I think they're *jealous* because Holly Agnew's coming. She's pretty, talented and famous. The Hi-Fives might be pretty and a little bit talented, but none of them are famous—at least not outside of Cedar River. The Hi-Fives like to be the center of attention. As long as Holly Agnew is in town, all the teenagers are going to be drawn to her."

"I think Binky might have something there," Jennifer agreed. "Minda wants to keep us wondering what she's going to do next. With Holly Agnew around, no one will care. No one will notice if Minda is wearing a fluorescent mini-skirt or a new pair of earrings. She doesn't like to share the spotlight with anyone."

"It's rude, rude, rude," Egg groaned.

Lexi, Jennifer, Binky and Todd all turned to stare at him. Egg was slumped against his seat looking pale and morose. He shook his head and moaned, "I mean *really* rude."

"What are you talking about, Egg?"

"It's so pathetic that the Hi-Fives are bored."

"Why should you care? You're not their entertainment committee," Binky pointed out.

"No, but I don't want to be the brunt of their pranks, either. When the Hi-Fives are bored, that usually means problems for anyone who gets in their way. We've seen it happen before. Remember the summer we were fourteen and the Hi-Fives played all those practical jokes on us?"

"Oh, that," Binky looked forlorn. "They called our house and told our mother that we'd been doing stuff like picking flowers out of other people's gardens and toilet-papering trees in yards." She rolled her eyes. "My mother was furious. We were grounded until we could convince her we weren't guilty."

"Like I said," moaned Egg, "if the Hi-Fives are bored, it means problems."

"Cheer up, guys," Lexi said. "I don't think they're all that bored. Even if they are, the tennis tournament is going to be of some interest to them. They just don't want to admit it. Can you imagine Minda passing up the opportunity to meet a real teenage tennis star? At least she'll be interested in the clothes she wears."

"I wonder what she'll look like in real life?" Binky asked. "She looks pretty in the magazines."

"She usually wears her hair in a pony tail," Todd said. "I suppose that keeps the hair out of her face when she's playing tennis."

"She never smiles when she's playing," Egg commented. "I wonder if that means she's crabby."

"Oh, Egg. That just means she's serious about what she does," Lexi said. "Besides, you've only seen her a few minutes on television. When she comes to Cedar River, she'll have lots of time off the court to show us her smile."

"I hope she likes it here," Todd interjected. "My coach is worried about that. Holly's father is a very wealthy man. He doesn't like it when his daughter is unhappy."

"What father does?" Lexi commented. "See? She's just like the rest of us. She has a dad who worries about her."

"You always try to look on the positive side," Binky pointed out. "But I'm afraid Holly might think of Cedar River the way the Hi-Fives do. She might find it boring!"

Todd slapped his palms on the table. "Then that'll be our next project, gang—making sure Holly Agnew likes Cedar River!"

Chapter Three

"Anybody home?" Todd poked his head through the Leighton's kitchen door.

Lexi handed him a bowl of cookie dough and a spoon. "Here, stir this," she ordered.

"What's going on?"

Across the room, Egg, Binky and Jennifer were dropping spoons of cookie dough onto baking sheets.

"I promised Mom I'd make something for the bake sale at church," Lexi explained. "We've formed an assembly line." She pointed at the bowl. "Stir."

"What are you doing here, Todd?" Egg asked. "I thought you had to work at your brother's garage this afternoon."

"I did, but he let me go early." Todd gave a vigorous swipe through the bowl. "I had to talk to my tennis coach, to see what his plans were for the tournament."

"Is there anything we should know?" Lexi wondered. "We're still going to work there, aren't we?"

"You bet. In fact, I learned some big news from the coach."

Binky's and Egg's eyes lit with curiosity. "What kind of news?"

"Have either of you ever been by the Hanson house on Sixth Street?"

"That huge, ancient thing at the top of the hill?"

"That's the one. Coach Barris told me that Holly Agnew and her coach are renting *that* house."

Egg's jaw dropped in surprise. "The haunted house?"

"Haunted?" Lexi looked from one friend to another, puzzled. "What do you mean 'haunted'?"

"Don't pay any attention to them, Lexi," Jennifer waved a hand in the air. "There isn't any such thing as a 'haunted' house. Especially not here in Cedar River."

"There is so," Binky said indignantly. "I've heard the stories about old Mr. Peter Hanson. It was his house. There was a terrible murder committed right there, and Mr. Hanson went insane."

"Wait a minute. You'd better slow down and start over. I want to hear this," Jennifer said.

"Cool it, Binky," Todd said with a laugh. "The Hanson house isn't haunted. The Hansons were a very eccentric family who lived in Cedar River for several generations. Peter Hanson, the youngest, died only a couple of years ago."

"What do you mean by 'eccentric'?" Lexi asked, still confused.

"Kooky, weird, spooky," Binky interjected. "All of those things."

"None of those things," Todd said. "Mr. Hanson was an inventor. He turned the basement of the house into a laboratory. According to my mom, he couldn't sleep very well at night so he'd go into the basement and tinker with his projects. Because he liked to do that sort of thing, he got a reputation for being odd.

"No one gave him credit for his creativity. They thought he was some sort of weirdo that stayed up all night trying to invent impossible things. He was a very shy man and didn't like to go out much. What made the stories worse was that his wife-to-be died under some unusual circumstances.

"After the death of his fiancee, Velda Martee, he became even more shy and reclusive. Mr. Hanson turned into a hermit. He didn't like to talk to people, so he came out only at night. Mom used to see him going for groceries at the twenty-four-hour supermarket. In later years, before his own death, he refused to go to town for anything. He did all his shopping through catalogs. He ordered his food by phone and the grocery delivered it to his door. The only people who ever saw him were the mailman and the delivery boy."

"How strange," Jennifer commented.

"Mother says it was a shame," Todd continued, "because he was really brilliant. He invented some clever things. He was working on a wind generator that he claimed would revolutionize the way we heat our homes. He also wrote books, and some nonconventional poetry. Mom says that when he died, Cedar River lost a true creative genius."

"It seems to me Cedar River lost one weird character." Binky was unimpressed. "That story makes me nervous. Why would anyone decide to stay inside and never go out except after dark?" Her eyes began to widen. "I'll bet he was a vampire! Daylight probably hurt his eyes and he had to go out at night to find victims. He'd plunge his fangs into their necks and drink their blood!"

"I think someone has plunged their fangs into your head and sucked out all your brain cells," Egg said. "How can you even imagine a story like that?"

"She's watched too many horror movies, that's all," Jennifer reasoned. "She's not rooted in reality anymore. Everybody's who's a little bit strange becomes a ghost or a vampire or some sort of extraterrestrial."

Binky stared blankly out the window at the backyard where Ben Leighton played with his rabbits. "I wonder if there are any ghosts in the Hanson house," she said dreamily. "After all, I've heard the rumor . . ."

"Rumors? What rumors?" Lexi's head was spinning.

"I've seen movies about ghosts," Binky commented. "They're really pretty creepy, don't you think?"

Jennifer gave a loud, unlady-like snort. "There are no such things as ghosts!"

"I don't know about that. Just because you can't see something doesn't mean it isn't there. Once I saw a movie about a ghost who came back to haunt someone who had wronged him before his death. He nearly drove the guy insane. It's a good thing the movie ended when it did."

"Binky, you don't believe everything you see in the theater, do you?"

"Oh, Lexi. You aren't any fun." Binky's lower lip projected in a pout. "Lighten up. You're just trying to change the subject."

"What *was* the subject?"

"That crazy Mr. Hanson and his haunted house," Binky said with ghoulish relish. "The *haunted* house in Cedar River."

"Tell me a little bit about the house itself," Lexi asked.

"It's huge." Egg gestured widely with his arms, indicating its vast size.

"And it's creepy," Jennifer added. "Even I have to admit that. And spooky people really did live there."

"The house does have a bad history," Todd admitted. "My mother remembers the place well. Apparently there was a lot of insanity in the family— before Mr. Hanson, that is."

Lexi swallowed hard. This was beginning to sound like a plot from one of Binky's horror movies. "Well, Mr. Hanson didn't sound so bad. What happened to his fiancee?"

"Velda was . . . uh . . . killed," Todd answered.

"Oh? How?" Lexi tried to remain nonchalant.

"She was stabbed to death by an intruder."

"How horrible!" Lexi gasped. "No wonder Mr. Hanson became a hermit. His heart must have been broken."

"She was killed in the Hanson house in an upstairs room. After Peter Hanson died, some kids sneaked into the house and looked through it. They told a story about a room upstairs stained with blood." Binky shuddered. "They said there was a huge stain in the middle of the hardwood floor and the curtains and walls were splattered."

"Binky, you're giving yourself the willies. Those

kids made up that story to scare everyone and you know it," Todd said.

"Maybe, maybe not. I've heard there's a ghost in that house."

Lexi and Todd both burst out laughing. "No way, Binky!"

But Binky seemed to enjoy scaring herself—thinking of the Hanson house and the tragic death that had occurred there.

"What really did happen to Velda Martee?" Lexi asked.

"The police said an intruder broke in, intending to rob the place," Todd explained. "Velda, who wasn't expected to be there, surprised him and he killed her."

"That doesn't seem scary," Lexi replied. "That seems pitiful and tragic."

Binky wrapped her arms around her own shoulders and hugged herself tightly. "Wouldn't it be neat to go to that house for Halloween? Ooooh, that would be scary. Just like the movies."

"You mean you actually think being afraid is thrilling?" Lexi asked.

"I guess you could say that," Binky admitted.

"What happens if the fear goes too far and it's not a thrill anymore?" Lexi asked pointedly.

"Don't even humor her with intelligent questions," Egg interrupted. "She's been watching too many stupid movies. Now, with Holly Agnew staying in the old Hanson house, we'll be hearing about spooks and ghosts and monsters the whole time."

The conversation was becoming more and more uncomfortable to Lexi. She knew her parents would rather she didn't see horror movies. Her mother always told Lexi that she shouldn't fill her mind with such things. The Leightons encouraged her to listen to good music and read wholesome books instead.

In the last year her parents had allowed Lexi to make her own choices concerning movies. She remembered her mother saying, "We've taught you right from wrong, good from evil. You know if something goes against your Christian beliefs. You're old enough to decide for yourself how you're going to handle it." As Lexi listened to Binky babble on about scary movies and haunted houses, she was extremely glad that her mother had taught her to be sensible about these things.

The buzzer went off in the kitchen. "Cookies are done," Lexi announced, glad for the interruption.

Just then, Lexi's little brother Ben burst through the back door. He was huffing and puffing with exertion. His eyes were wide and he looked frightened.

"Ben, what's wrong?"

"There are spooks outside, Lexi. They're in the trees."

"Spooks?" Lexi asked with a sinking sensation in her stomach. "What do you mean?"

"They make sounds like this." Ben made an odd, grating sound in his throat.

"Are you sure you're not hearing the wind in the branches?" Todd asked Ben.

"Wind. Branches." Ben echoed. "Spooky."

"Come on, little guy. Let's go check it out." Todd took Ben by the hand and led him outside. Unfortunately, Ben's fears only reminded Binky of the subject Lexi didn't want to discuss. She continued her chatter about haunted houses.

"It seems strange that Holly Agnew would want to rent the Hanson house. Why would anyone want to live in a house that has such a horrible reputation?"

"Maybe Holly doesn't know about the house's reputation," Jennifer pointed out. "It really is a beautiful home. It's very large, with grand staircases, and several windows overlooking the pretty gardens. There's also a turret on the front of the house with a really neat lookout balcony."

"And it's still in good shape even though no one's living there?" Lexi asked.

"A real estate agency has been trying to sell the house for some time. They keep it clean and have the gardens trimmed and cared for. They know it will be easier to sell if it's kept up." Jennifer looked thoughtful. "Frankly, if I didn't know the story behind the house, I'd like to live there myself."

"Well, I think Holly Agnew should be warned," Binky said indignantly. "Her coach is bringing her into a very scary place."

Todd returned to the kitchen. "Just some birds chirping in the trees," he chuckled. He'd reassured Ben that there were no "spooks" and left him in the yard to play with his rabbits.

"Jennifer and Binky were telling me more about the Hanson house," Lexi explained.

"It's really a beautiful old mansion," Todd acknowledged. "I think the reason it hasn't sold is because they're asking too much."

"I think it hasn't sold because it's haunted," Binky insisted. "It's really sad that a famous person like Holly Agnew has to stay in a haunted house."

Late that afternoon, when the cookies were baked and conversation was exhausted, Lexi's friends left. It was clear that each of them was imagining how it would be for superstar tennis player, Holly Agnew, to arrive in Cedar River and move into the large and frightening house on the hill.

Chapter Four

Lexi awoke with a start. She was sweating, her legs were tangled in the sheets, and she was clutching her pillow so tightly her knuckles were white. Slowly, muscle by muscle, Lexi relaxed. Finally, she lay back against the pillows and expelled a long sigh of relief. It had only been a dream, a nightmare. Lexi closed her eyes, glad for the early morning sun falling across her bed, taking the chill from the room.

She'd dreamed about the house on the hill. In her dream, Frankenstein's monster had taken residence in the house. In the dark of night, the monster would search graveyards for body parts with which to make his half-human creations. When he'd exhausted all his resources, he stood over her bed, staring greedily down at her.

Lexi had had some frightening dreams before, of course, but they were always about riding on a runaway roller coaster or becoming lost in a dark forest. Never had her dreams been about flesh-hungry monsters.

She had Binky and that silly movie to thank for this. Lexi pulled the blankets up to her chin, feeling cold in spite of the sun streaming in the window. The movie had left her feeling tarnished. It had put thoughts into her mind that hadn't been there before—frightening, upsetting thoughts. Lexi didn't like it at all.

She hurried with her shower and dressed quickly. Mrs. Leighton was in the kitchen stirring a large saucepan of oatmeal with raisins when Lexi entered the room.

"Good morning, sweetheart. Did you sleep well?"

"No, I didn't, actually," Lexi admitted. "I had a terrible night."

"That doesn't sound like you, Lexi. You usually sleep like a log."

"I had a horrible dream."

Mrs. Leighton covered the pan and pulled out a chair at the kitchen table. "Sit down, Lexi. Tell me about it."

Lexi felt foolish now, with bright light streaming through the windows and the cheerful sounds and smells of her mother's kitchen. "I don't know. Maybe it wasn't so bad . . ."

"Nightmares always sound bad to me," Mrs. Leighton prodded.

"It was stupid, now that I think about it," Lexi said with a forced smile. "There was a monster who was looking for body parts. He'd been to all the graveyards in Cedar River, and finally came to our house for parts of me."

"What a dreadful dream!" Mrs. Leighton exclaimed. "I wonder where that came from."

"Oh, I know exactly where it came from," Lexi said ruefully. She explained about the horror movie she and the others had seen, and how much Binky loved them. She also told her mother that Holly Agnew's coach had rented the Hanson house, and how Binky was sure it was haunted.

"I've never liked those awful movies, and they seem to be so popular these days." Mrs. Leighton frowned. "The main reason I don't like them is that they fill your mind with unpleasant thoughts and ideas. In an almost manipulative way they seem to make violence acceptable—legitimate. Does that make sense to you, Lexi?"

"Until yesterday, I might have laughed at you, Mom. If you'd told me seeing such movies was harmful, I probably would have argued the point. At first, it didn't seem that seeing some violence, some terror, some fake blood, would have any effect on me. But this morning, I'm not so sure. It was a pretty ugly dream I had last night."

"This is a bit of a coincidence," Mrs. Leighton said with a light laugh, "but I happened to be reading the story of creation this morning in my devotional time."

"Oh? What does that have to do with horror movies?"

"The wonderful thing about the Garden of Eden before the fall was that it existed in a state of perfect harmony—God's harmony. Man, the plants and animals all lived together in perfect unity. There was no violence, no pain, no death."

"It's too bad we lost that, isn't it Mom?" Lexi commented sadly. "It would be great to live in a place where violence didn't exist."

"Yes it would," Lexi's mother agreed. "Now it seems that violence, pain and death are commonplace—in movie theaters, even in picture books for children. All that evil and corruption go against the very core of our creation. God created a world of peace and harmony. Somehow, we've managed to turn it into a place where violence and cruelty are considered entertainment. We've allowed ourselves to become victimized. It shows in the type of movies we watch."

"I'd never thought of it that way," Lexi admitted.

"Frankly, I believe horror movies are just the beginning."

"The beginning of what?"

"The beginning of the end of our humanity, our generosity and our compassion for others. These movies and so many things we see on TV make us numb to people's needs. If we see people slashed to death on the screen and can walk away laughing, what will be our reaction the next time we see someone injured in real life—a small child with a scraped knee, or an elderly person who's fallen? Will we respond with indifference instead of compassion? I'm afraid our society is going to become unaffected by people who are truly frightened or hurting. We shouldn't be able to see violence and not have a deep and strong reaction against it."

"You're scaring me, Mom. How come you've never told me any of this before?"

"I suppose because it never came up, Lexi. Now that you've seen for yourself the effect of seeing such violence on the screen, it seems the time to talk about it."

"I don't feel numb or uncaring about others just because I saw that movie yesterday," Lexi said. "Are you sure it works that way?"

"Perhaps one movie isn't going to do it. But, if you subject yourself to negative things over and over, eventually it's bound to have a negative effect on you."

"I suppose you're right, Mom."

"It seems that young people tend to want a slightly bigger thrill, a little more fun, than they had the last time," Mrs. Leighton went on, as if Lexi hadn't responded. "If you saw the same movie again, would you be as frightened by it the second time?"

"Of course not. I'd know what was coming."

"Exactly. If you really wanted to be frightened again, you'd have to look for something a little more violent. It's not wise to seek one thrill after another." Mrs. Leighton wiped her hand across her forehead. "I'm lecturing, aren't I? Sorry, Lexi."

A small stirring at the entrance to the kitchen made them both turn. Ben stood in the doorway in his pajamas, clutching his blanket and teddy bear to his chest. His dark silky hair was spiked and tousled, his brown eyes round and dark as chocolate.

"How long have you been standing here, Benjamin?" Mrs. Leighton asked with concern.

Ben stuck his thumb in his mouth and mumbled. "Scary."

Mrs. Leighton sighed. "Too long, I see."

Ben crawled onto a kitchen chair while his mother dished up a bowl of the steaming oatmeal. She also filled Lexi's bowl.

"I didn't feel like eating last night, but today I feel much better," Lexi admitted as she swallowed a spoonful. "That silly Binky had me so worked up . . .

I shouldn't have spent any time thinking about that movie, but then it was the Hanson house that was on my mind. Yesterday, everyone was saying that a murder had been committed in that house. That's why Mr. Hanson became such a recluse and an eccentric."

"Oh? I didn't realize that," Mrs. Leighton remarked. "All I know is that it's a lovely home. Old, but kept in good shape."

"Don't you think it's kind of spooky-looking?" Lexi asked.

"Some people think Victorian mansions in general have that look. Personally, I think they're beautiful." Mrs. Leighton sat down at the table with her cereal. "I like the gables, turrets and gingerbread trim. In fact, I wouldn't mind living in a house like that. I wonder if the Hanson house is for sale . . ."

"No!" Lexi was surprised at the agitated tone of her own voice. "You don't want that house, Mom."

"Lexi, you don't actually believe the house is haunted, do you?"

"No—I guess not, not really," Lexi stammered. She felt herself beginning to relax. Her mother was always so logical. "You're right, Mom, as usual. That stupid movie really messed me up."

Mrs. Leighton stood up from the table, and spoke to her son, "Well, Benjamin. Should we work in the garden this morning?"

"You bet!" Ben's spoon flipped out of his bowl and onto the floor. "Ooops." He scrambled to pick it up. "I'll get dressed. We can plant flowers!"

Lexi had just placed some dishes in the dishwasher when Binky burst through the door. Her cheeks were pink and her eyes were wild, her red hair looked like a flaming torch atop her head. She waved her hands and bounced on the balls of her feet. "Lexi, Lexi, wait until you hear this!" she squealed.

"What *is* it, Binky?"

"Is this a coincidence or what?" Binky asked dramatically.

"I don't understand what you're talking about."

"Only yesterday we were talking about the haunted house up on the hill, right?" Binky said, her voice patient, almost condescending. "And Todd told us Holly Agnew was planning to rent it. Now, today, the very day after hearing that news, strange things have begun to happen."

"Don't tell me. The ghosts have written a letter to the mayor in protest," Lexi said sarcastically. She punched the wash cycle on the dishwasher. "Or maybe they're picketing outside the mayor's office— 'No More Renters.' Or are the signs invisible, like the ghosts?"

"I know you're making fun of me, Lexi, but some really strange things *have* begun to happen."

"What kinds of things?" Binky was getting on her nerves.

Binky's eyes sparkled with anticipation at the thought of imparting her news. "Has anyone in your family been uptown this morning?"

"My dad went to work, but the rest of us have been in the house."

"All the flags in town are flying upside down, Lexi! The only one right-side-up is in front of the haunted house."

"The Hanson house," Lexi corrected her friend, "and what do you mean?"

"Just what I said. The flags. They're upside down."

"No one in Cedar River leaves the United States flag up overnight."

"Not those flags. The 'Welcome to Cedar River' flags that are up on every block. They're all upside down. Weird, huh?"

Lexi was unimpressed. "It's just pranksters. Someone playing a joke." She smiled. "It's rather funny, too. It must have been a lot of work to turn all those flags upside down."

"You think it's a joke?"

"Of course it is. What else could it be?"

"I think it's a signal. A sign. Doesn't it seem odd to you that the only flag in town that wasn't turned upside down is the one in front of the haunted house?"

"The Hanson house, Binky," Lexi corrected again. "It's not haunted."

"Whatever. Don't you think it's odd?"

"Maybe the prankster forgot that one."

"I think the ghosts did it."

Lexi stared at her friend in disbelief. "Binky, you're slipping over the edge."

"Well, maybe not ghosts, but evil people at least."

"Oh, at least," Lexi said sarcastically.

"I think someone wants Holly Agnew to stay out of that house," Binky said emphatically. "They're trying to tell her to go away."

"How long did it take you to think this one up, Binky?" Lexi turned to the counter to hide her smile. "You're too much."

Binky sat with her legs crossed beneath her, her

elbows resting on the table, her chin in her hands. "Nobody wants to believe me, but I know I'm right," she said dejectedly. "No one wants to admit that something strange is going on at that house. Doesn't anyone remember that a *murder* took place there?"

"That was a long time ago, Binky. Todd explained the situation. An eccentric old man lived there. Just because a murder took place doesn't mean people are going to be killed there again—and certainly not that it is inhabited by ghosts."

"I suppose not," Binky said reluctantly. "But it seems to me that if there's a mysterious house where someone was killed there must be a ghost hanging around somewhere."

———

Tournament week finally came. Lexi was busy at the clubhouse. "Have we stapled enough flyers yet?" she stared at the huge stacks before her.

"Let's do five hundred more. We don't want to run out."

Lexi was pleased to be around the tournament celebrities who were now arriving by the carload. She'd never seen so many famous and important people in one place in her entire life. There were camera crews and news reporters everywhere. The stars themselves, their families, and the fans who loved to watch them were all thrilling to see.

A flurry of noise and activity at the entrance drew Lexi's attention. An attractive teenage girl strode through the doorway. Her movements were brisk and precise. Her skin was clear and radiant, her hair dark and shiny. She had a ready smile at the sight of the young people. Lexi knew this had to be Holly Agnew.

Following her like a shadow was a tall, slender man. His shoulders were slightly stooped, and his eyes were dark and sunken above gaunt cheeks.

"There she is," Todd whispered to Lexi.

"Who's the creepy-looking fellow behind her?"

Todd's eyebrows disappeared beneath his mop of blond hair. "That's Anatoli Weare, Holly Agnew's coach."

Lexi stared at the sour man. He appeared as sullen and brooding as Holly was cheerful and vivacious. The more widely Holly smiled, greeting the people around her, the more grim her coach appeared.

"Todd! Lexi! Why don't you come over here and meet one of our best players," Coach Barris called.

Awestruck, Lexi and Todd moved toward the sparkling girl and her entourage.

"Lexi, Todd, this is the young woman you've been waiting to meet, Holly Agnew. Holly, I'd like to introduce two of our hardest workers, Lexi Leighton and Todd Winston."

"Great to meet you," Holly said brightly. "So you've been working on the tourney? I've heard from several of the players that it's very well organized. We're both glad to be here, aren't we, Tony?" She turned to the tall, brooding man behind her. "This is my coach, Anatoli Weare." Holly grinned impishly. "We call him Tony, for obvious reasons."

The tall man didn't smile. Lexi felt a wave of sympathy for Holly, who had to spend so much time with such a grim person. Of course if he were as fine a tennis coach as Todd said he was, his disposition hardly mattered, only his teaching skills.

Tony hovered very closely to Holly, as if he were watching her, making sure she didn't do anything out of character or against her strict training. To her surprise, Lexi felt a stab of dislike for the tall, dark man. Holly, however, seemed oblivious to his manner.

"I can't tell you how glad I am to meet someone my own age," she said with a winning smile. "There are a few young people on the circuit, but I get so tired of being the only *teenager*." Holly lowered herself into a chair near the table where Lexi and Todd had been working. "So, tell me, what's been happening in Cedar River?"

That was the last question they'd expected to hear from someone as important and famous as Holly.

"You'd think it was pretty boring, I'm sure," Lexi said.

"Try me," Holly replied. "You might be surprised."

Enthusiastically, Lexi and Todd began to recount the "Save Cedar River" project, their recycling campaign, and Egg's personal project to put a brick in every toilet. Before they were finished, Holly was laughing so hard tears brimmed her eyes.

"You mean you really have a friend named 'Egg'?" she asked.

"Actually, his name is Edward McNaughton, but Egg seems to fit him better," Todd explained.

"I have to meet this guy."

"He's got a sister named Binky who would love

to meet you too," Lexi offered.

"Binky and Egg. What terrific names! I can hardly wait."

Lexi was impressed with Holly's cheerfulness and her maturity. Besides that, Holly was even prettier than Lexi had expected she would be. Suddenly, from a few feet away, came Tony's emphatic voice, "You'll do what I say and that's final."

Holly glanced sharply in her coach's direction. A wave of unhappiness spread over her face. Her expression startled Lexi. Until then, Holly had seemed a poised, pleasant and completely happy young girl. Now, Lexi could detect a darker side. Her coach and his staff were bickering loudly.

In a sudden movement, Holly motioned Todd and Lexi to the far side of the room.

"Sorry about that," she whispered. "I hate it when they fight."

"Is there something wrong?" Lexi asked.

"Not as far as the tournament goes," Holly seemed certain. "They're fighting over the house we rented here in Cedar River."

"The Hanson house?" Todd asked.

"You know about it?" Holly seemed surprised.

"You're well-known, Holly," he explained. "When someone like you comes to town, everyone gets in on all the details."

"I guess I should be used to it by now, but I'm not. My coach likes the house. It has plenty of rooms, lots of privacy, and best of all, a private tennis court in back. He wants me to be able to do my warm-up exercises and a little practicing out there."

"That seems logical," Todd commented.

"I guess so. It's just that my tutor, Mr. Ivan, doesn't like it."

"Why's that?" Lexi asked.

"That's what they've been bickering about. Mr. Ivan says it gives him the creeps. He's never complained before and Tony doesn't like it."

"What do *you* want to do?" Todd wondered.

"I'll do whatever Tony says," Holly said matter-of-factly. "He's made me into a star. I can't stop listening to him now. Besides, he thinks it's the greatest house we've ever rented. But there is something about it . . ." Holly didn't explain.

"So you've heard the rumors already?"

"That was the first bit of local gossip—that the house had been the scene of a murder. They made it sound like the whole house is filled with haunts, spooks and ghosts. I even wondered about it myself. I thought we'd be tripping over poltergeists as we entered the place." Holly gave a weak grin. "It made me feel a little creepy."

"Can you put your finger on anything in particular about the house that makes you feel uncomfortable?" Lexi asked.

"Not really. I just don't like the idea of being in a house where a murder was committed. I hope I don't wake up every time I hear a creaking floorboard or wind in the trees." Holly chuckled. "Listen to me! I'm going to scare myself just talking about it. Isn't that silly?"

Lexi was glad that Binky wasn't around to hear what Holly had to say about the house.

Tony broke away from the group of bickering agents and moved toward Holly. "I have business calls to make," he said, his voice cool. "Would you like some free time while I take care of them?"

Holly nodded eagerly. It was obvious to Lexi that she didn't get much time alone away from her coach.

"If you're free, Holly," Lexi offered, "we could take you for a drive around town and show you the sights in Cedar River."

Holly looked to Tony for his approval. His dark gaze scrutinized Todd and Lexi thoroughly before he nodded.

Lexi felt like she'd barely passed a difficult test. Tony Weare was an alarming and intimidating man. She was glad she didn't have to work with him.

"You really don't mind?" Holly asked excitedly. "Are you sure you have time to bother with me?"

"Bother with you?" Todd laughed. "You're the biggest news in Cedar River. It'll be fun just to drive around town with you and watch our friends turn green with envy."

Holly giggled. "What a lovely thing to say. But, if you don't mind, I think I'll wear sunglasses and a hat so no one recognizes me."

For a moment, Lexi felt a wave of compassion for a girl so young and yet so famous she had to disguise herself so as not to attract a crowd.

Chapter Five

In the parking lot, Holly made a beeline for Todd's '49 Ford Coupe. "Neat car!" she exclaimed, running her hand over the chrome. "Who does it belong to?"

"It's mine," Todd said proudly. "I've been fixing it up for the last two years."

"I like the old ones myself. No plastic. Besides that, I hate to drive by junkyards and see old cars piled up." Holly rapped her knuckles on the hood. "Good job."

Holly Agnew couldn't have said anything that would have pleased Todd more. Lexi knew that Holly had made a friend.

"There must be a lot of older blue cars in this town," Holly remarked, gazing across the lot.

"Why do you say that?" Lexi hadn't noticed many old blue cars around besides Todd's.

"Look at that one." Holly pointed toward an old car, the body rusted in several spots. It was quite ugly, but the very same color blue as Todd's. "I've seen several cars just like that one all over Cedar River."

Todd frowned. "That's strange. I don't remember

seeing any cars like that at the garage."

"That one looks like it's never been to a garage!" Holly remarked with a laugh.

"Are you sure you haven't seen the *same* car everywhere?" Todd wondered.

"Could be," Holly admitted. "I don't pay much attention to things like that. It just seems strange to me that a rickety old car like that one would turn up wherever I was." It was an odd bit of information. Holly laughed lightly and shrugged it off. "Did I hear someone say they'd give me a tour of this town?"

Todd opened the door to his car. "Your carriage is waiting, ladies."

"Listen to him," Holly said. "Who does he think he is? Prince Charming?"

They chattered like old friends as they drove around Cedar River. Todd took them past the park where they had all worked so hard, and they told Holly more about the environmental project to beautify the city. Then they drove by the nursing home where Lexi's grandmother lived, and by the Hamburger Shack where the gang hung out.

Holly also requested to see the mall, and the high school Todd and Lexi attended. On the way back to the tennis courts she suggested, "Why don't we drive by the Hanson mansion? I'll give you a tour."

"Really?" Lexi gasped.

"Why not? Everybody's talking about the house. You might as well see it for yourselves."

Lexi and Todd stared at the house as they pulled into the winding driveway. It was a regal old Victorian with several porches and gables.

"It doesn't look so bad," Lexi remarked. "I

thought it would be covered with old vines or spider webs or something."

"Oh no. It's been kept up beautifully. My coach had his own cleaning crew come through as well before we arrived. All the windows are spotless and the floors gleam."

Todd and Lexi followed Holly eagerly through the front door. Lexi expected at least a hinge to creak as they opened the door. Instead, it opened smoothly. The rooms inside were very impressive. The ceilings were nine feet high, and all the woodwork was dark and rich.

"Stained-glass windows, too!" Todd exclaimed. "Nice."

"And hardwood floors." Lexi could practically see her reflection in the shine.

"It's too bad it's so dark in here," Todd said. "It could use a few more windows."

"I agree. It's a great house, but gloomy." Holly walked them through the formal parlor and the main dining room to the kitchen. "This is the worst part of the house," she said with a sweeping gesture. "The kitchen hasn't been updated. Fortunately, we never cook. Tony has everything catered. He watches my diet very carefully, but occasionally, when he's busy with something else," her voice lowered to a whisper, "I order a pizza."

Holly chattered about her life on tour as casually and nonchalantly as Lexi and Binky might talk about school. She led them through each of the rooms of the house and up the back staircase. They reached a bright, sunny room near the very top.

"This is where I'm staying," she said. "Not bad, huh?"

The room had a large bay window complete with a window seat. A big four-poster bed with a thick velvet canopy stood on one wall, with a fireplace across from it. On either side of the fireplace were two massive bookshelves filled with old, leather-bound volumes.

"This was Mr. Hanson's room," Holly explained. She pointed to the books. "There's lots of scientific stuff in there. I took a couple of books out just to look at them." An odd expression crossed her features. "Can you keep a secret?"

"S-Sure," Lexi stammered.

"I mean a really *big* secret. I don't want Tony to hear of it."

"Should you be keeping secrets from your coach?" Todd asked.

Holly waved her hand. "Oh, it's nothing so bad," she said. "It's just that Tony's so strange about wanting to know where I am every minute, and every detail of my life. Sometimes I feel like I need something private—some part of me he can't control. Do you understand what I mean?"

Todd and Lexi nodded simultaneously. "We can keep your secret, Holly," Todd assured her.

"Come here, then." Holly moved toward the fireplace. "The books on the left are mostly fiction," Holly explained. "Mr. Hanson must have liked poetry. And he *loved* Shakespeare and Edgar Allen Poe." She ran her fingers across the spines of the books. "On the right side there are lots of scientific journals. I was curious about these because I'd heard Mr. Hanson was an inventor." Her hand touched a stiff volume. She pulled lightly and as if by magic, the bookcase swung out from the wall to reveal a dark, gaping hole.

"Holly! What have you done?"

Holly giggled and stepped back. "It's a secret passage. Isn't it great?"

"You found this?" Todd's voice crackled with amazement.

"Weird, huh?" Holly was delighted with the discovery. "I'd always heard about old houses with secret passageways and mysterious staircases. I knew there must be one in here somewhere. When Tony told me this had been Mr. Hanson's bedroom, I was sure that if there were a passage, it would have to be from his room. It took nearly two hours of pulling on books and feeling for unusual surfaces to discover this." She tapped the hard volume. "It's a fake. It covers a door latch. When you pull on it, the bookcase swings out from the wall."

"What's behind it?" Lexi moved a little closer to the black hole.

"Stairs." Holly peered into the blackness. "I have not asked for a flashlight. Tony would be too suspicious. That's why I wanted to show this to you. Maybe you guys could get me a flashlight. Then another day, when Tony and the gang aren't around, we can take a look down there."

Todd tried the first step. It creaked painfully. "We'll need light all right. I don't know how sturdy these steps are. This house is pretty old."

"What do you think it leads to, Todd?" Lexi asked, her voice breathless.

"The logical place is the basement. That's where Mr. Hanson had his work room." He peered again into the darkness. "He probably had it built specially for himself. They said he was eccentric."

"Isn't this great? Will you help me explore it when Tony's not around?" Holly's face fell. "If he found out about it, he'd have me moved out of this room. Tony has no imagination. He's not a lot of fun. He's probably the world's best tennis coach, but frankly, he doesn't want me thinking about anything except tennis."

"How dull," Lexi agreed.

"I know. That's why I want you to keep this passage a secret. It'll be something for me to think about. Something for us to explore. Do you mind? Will you help me?"

How could Todd and Lexi turn her down? "Sure!"

"Thanks, guys. I really appreciate it. For now, we'd better close this up." Holly pushed the bookshelf back into place. The latch clicked. "You'd never know it's there, would you?" Holly asked, looking at the fireplace and matching bookshelves.

"Not in a million years," Lexi agreed.

"I'm going to write to my parents and tell them about this door. They'll get a big kick out of it."

"Tell us about your parents, Holly. You haven't mentioned them," Todd asked.

An expression of longing and loneliness crossed Holly's features. "I miss them. They're on a big trip. My dad had to go abroad. They're going to Tokyo, London, Paris and then they're coming here to Cedar River. They should arrive before the end of the tourney. My dad is an international lawyer. He does a lot of business between the United States and other countries. It's difficult with my parents going in one direction and me another. That's why they like Tony so much, though," Holly said. "He's careful about what I do and where I go. They know he takes good care of me."

"Do you like Tony?" Lexi asked.

"He's all right. He doesn't have much of a sense of humor, but some of the other guys in my entourage do. Especially the bodyguard."

"If you have a bodyguard, why isn't he following you right now?" Lexi wondered.

"I asked him not to. His real job is to stay by me during the tournament when there are big crowds. Otherwise he pretty much lets me be on my own." Holly glanced from Todd to Lexi and back again. "He didn't think you two looked like a danger to me, or would spirit me off somewhere to hold me for ransom!"

"I don't envy your life, Holly," Lexi said, shaking her head. "It sounds too hard."

"But exciting," Todd added.

"Sometimes I wish I could be a normal teenager going to a normal high school." Holly made an imaginary swing with a tennis racket. "But then, I wouldn't be able to play the game I love the most."

At that moment, Lexi realized how much she liked Holly Agnew. She was smart, mature, sensible and fun to be around.

"Before we go back to the clubhouse and Tony keeps me busy, I'd like to take a walk by the river. You've talked so much about all the work you've done down there, I think I should see the place for myself."

They hurried downstairs and through the house, paying little attention to the ornate but somewhat heavy atmosphere of the rooms. They exited into the sunshine and piled into Todd's car for the drive to the park.

"There's the gazebo." Lexi pointed to a large white gingerbread structure. "In the summer, various bands perform concerts there. Sometimes we bring a blanket or picnic lunch and listen to them."

"I hope they do that while I'm here," Holly said wistfully. "And that Tony will let me attend."

As they moved toward the center of the park, Lexi noticed a large group of people milling about. There were several anxious faces in the crowd. Lexi gasped and put her hand to her mouth. "Todd! Look!"

Something very strange had happened in the park!

Chapter Six

Todd quickly pulled off the road and they all jumped out of the car.

"Something's happening around old Hannibal T. Jameson," Lexi remarked.

"Who's Hannibal T. Jameson?" Holly asked.

"He's the fellow who founded this town over a hundred years ago," Lexi explained. "The real name of the park is the H. T. Jameson Park, but everyone calls it Cedar River Park. There's always been a joke about the statue."

"Right," Todd said with a grin. "Old Hannibal T. has done more for the pigeons in this region than he ever did for the townspeople. But he's collecting quite a crowd right now. Let's go over and see what's going on."

They hurried across the grass. "That's odd," Lexi exclaimed, "the statue looks shorter."

"Well, I should think so," Holly said. "Or has the head always been missing?"

As they neared the crowd, they could see only a metal post protruding from the bronze statue. "Looks like someone popped the head right off," Todd said.

"At least they didn't go too far with it." Holly

pointed toward a nearby stump. The head of the famous founder sat on top of it. Two policemen were
bending to examine it.

Then Lexi heard a high-pitched squeal near the
center of the crowd. "It's ghosts. It's ghosts. Somebody took off its head. Remember the story of the
headless horseman? Now we have a headless statue
right here in Cedar River. This park is haunted, I'm
sure of it."

"Do you hear what I hear?" Lexi muttered.

Todd nodded and closed his eyes. Together, they
mouthed the name, "Binky."

"What's that?" Holly asked.

"Hear the high-pitched voice in the middle of the
crowd?" Todd said with a grimace. "Well, that's
Binky—she's the one with the brother named Egg."

Holly tilted her head and listened.

"That's what Binky sounds like when she's freaking out," Lexi explained.

"And she freaks out quite regularly," Todd added.
"As you can tell, she's quite an expert."

Just then, Binky broke through the crowd and
came darting toward them. "Lexi! Todd! Did you see
what happened to old Jameson's head? Isn't it weird?
Just like in the movie. I saw this horror flick about
a monster who could never leave heads alone. Of
course, they were attached to real people, but—"

"Binky, if you'd calm down for just a minute, I'd
like to introduce you to Holly Agnew."

Binky stopped jabbering at once. Her jaw dropped
and she stared in awe. "The *real* Holly Agnew?"

Holly grinned and pinched herself. "Yup, I'm
real."

"Oh, it's so nice to meet you," Binky said. She pumped Holly's hand vigorously. "Isn't it terrible that you had to come at such a time?"

"What's wrong with now, Binky?"

"Oh, all these weird and spooky things are happening around Cedar River. First the flags. Now the statue." She turned to Holly with solemn eyes. "I think Cedar River is haunted. I'm sorry you had to get involved in this."

"This is obviously the work of pranksters, Binky," Lexi murmured. She didn't want Holly to think poorly of Cedar River.

But Binky wouldn't let it go at that. "You're staying in the Hanson house, aren't you? That's haunted too, you know. I realize it's an awfully pretty house, but it's definitely haunted. There was a murder committed there. A bloody, gory murder. The man who lived there was eccentric. He worked in his basement inventing things. Have you found any of his inventions yet? Is there anything weird in the house?"

"What exactly do you mean by weird?" Holly glanced knowingly at Todd and Lexi.

"Blood stains. Furniture that moves by itself. Strange noises in the attic. You know, stuff like that. Knives out of place . . ."

"You didn't ask about axes and chain saws, Binky," Todd said with a laugh.

Binky gave him a disgusted look. "I'm just asking. I have to know."

"Sorry, Binky," Holly played along. "Whoever the murderer was, he was very neat. The worst thing I found was a mousetrap with the cheese half-eaten."

"Ooooh, mice. Gross!"

"Binky, you're too much," Todd said. "You're the only person I know who gets equally excited about chain-saw massacres and mice." He put his arm around her thin shoulders. "Come on. Why don't you come to the Hamburger Shack with us? We can discuss this mysterious beheading over a burger and some fries."

Binky looked wistfully at the decapitated statue. "Well, I suppose. I have to go there anyway to meet Egg."

"Can you come along, Holly?" Lexi asked hopefully.

"I'd love to. I'm having more fun today than I've had in the last three weeks on tour. You don't know how lucky you are to live normal lives and to be able to do whatever you want on a summer day like this."

"But, you're famous," Binky pointed out.

"True, but fame isn't always fun."

Lexi felt sorry for Holly. She was always in the public eye because of her tennis and because of her father's wealth. There was no way she could be a normal teen. Lexi felt no envy for Holly's status or her lifestyle. In fact, Lexi gave a brief prayer of thanks for the normalcy of her own life.

"I'm so hungry, I could eat a dozen burgers," Binky announced as they climbed into Todd's car. She chattered happily in the backseat on the way to the Hamburger Shack.

Egg was waiting inside at the group's usual table. "There you are." He frowned at his sister. "You're late. What happened to you?"

"The most exciting thing in the world!" Binky enthused. With a bit of exaggeration, she told Egg about the decapitated statue in the park.

Egg was not impressed. "It's a prank, Binky. Even *you* should be able to see that."

"I don't think it is, Egg. Something strange is going on in this town."

At that moment, Jerry Randall came to take their order.

"Jerry, I'd like you to meet our friend Holly Agnew," Lexi said, glad for the interruption. "She's the tennis star who's come to play in the Cedar River tournament."

Jerry was impressed. "Really? I've heard about you. You're supposed to be great."

Holly laughed self-consciously and lowered her eyes. "Let's hope so. That's what my coach is counting on."

Jerry glanced around the room. There were no other customers. "Do you mind if I sit down and talk a minute?" he asked. "I'd really like to hear about your life. It must be interesting to travel around, playing in all these towns."

"Sounds better than it is," Holly admitted. "Sometimes I'd like nothing better than to be just like you guys. Staying in one place. Going to high school with my friends. Having a regular boyfriend. All that stuff."

Jerry pulled up a chair and sat down beside Holly. Lexi could sense the immediate attraction between them. Jerry was more talkative than normal, obviously trying to impress Holly.

"How long have you worked here, Jerry?"

"It seems like forever."

"It's a neat old place. Has it always been a teen hangout?"

"As long as I can remember," Todd said.

"No, not always," Jerry corrected. "There was another business conducted here before it became the Hamburger Shack. My boss told me about it."

"Really? What was it before?" Binky wondered.

"It was a funeral home," Jerry answered, looking evenly at Binky.

Binky's eyes grew wide. "You're kidding, right? I've been eating at a funeral home all these years?"

"Honest." Jerry smiled at Binky and his eyes twinkled.

She shook her head emphatically. "You're kidding. You know I'm squeamish and you're teasing me."

"It would be a great joke to play on you, Binky, but I'm not. This was a funeral home."

"I don't believe you," Binky crossed her arms and thrust her jaw out at a stubborn angle.

"I could prove it if you want me to."

"You're lying."

Jerry pushed away from the table and stood up. He went into the kitchen where the gang could see him talking with his boss. After a moment, the older man nodded his head and Jerry returned to the lunchroom. He removed his apron and folded it across a chair. "Come on, Binky—and anyone else who doesn't believe me."

"What are you going to do?"

"I'm going to give you a ride in the elevator that used to carry caskets up from the basement."

"Caskets? Ooooh, gross. You're making this up, Jerry Randall."

"You're the one who didn't believe me, Binky. You're the one who needs the proof."

Todd motioned to Lexi, Holly and Egg. "Come on. I've got to see this."

They trailed through a storage room filled with containers of catsup, mustard, napkins and plastic spoons. At the very back of the building, along the side wall, were two large doors bolted together.

"There it is."

"That's nothing," Binky said with a pout. "That's just a plain old closet."

"No, it isn't. There's an elevator in there. See this?" Jerry pointed to some faint marks on the back wall. "There used to be a garage door here. The hearse would pull in and they'd lift the caskets up from the basement."

"Oh, Jerry Randall, quit it! You're just being icky. You're trying to scare me." Binky huffed.

"Me?" Jerry looked hurt. "You're the one who didn't believe me. Do you want a ride in the elevator?"

"That's no elevator and you're just fooling . . ." Binky's voice trailed away as Jerry took the key out of his pocket, unlocked the padlock and flung the doors open to reveal a long, narrow, hand-driven elevator. When he opened the door, a flood of stale, musty air permeated the room.

"Oh! It is," Binky gasped.

"Go on, Binky. Take a ride. I dare you. You're the one who started all of this." Egg poked his sister in the back and nudged her a little closer to the open doors.

"What's downstairs?"

"Just a storage area," Jerry assured her.

"Go on, Binky. Take a ride." Egg pushed her closer. "I dare you."

"I don't have to listen to you, Egg McNaughton."

"I *double* dare you, Binky."

With a huff and a frown, Binky moved toward the elevator. Then her bravado wavered. "Is somebody going to go down with me?"

"I will," Jerry said with a sly grin. "I have to work the elevator from the inside."

"Who says I trust you, Jerry Randall?" Binky said with her hands on her hips.

"You don't dare, huh?"

"Oh, all right. But there'd better not be anything terrible down there. It's just a storage room, right?"

"Honest," Jerry said, his eyes betraying nothing.

Nervously, Binky stepped over the ledge and into the elevator. Jerry jumped in behind her and worked at the ropes and pulleys along the side. With a screeching squeal, the elevator started to move. Binky's own scream pitched with the sound of the long unused pulleys.

Lexi shivered. "What a terrible sound."

"Worse than fingernails on a chalkboard," Holly agreed.

Binky's squeals and screams were coming from the rapidly lowering elevator. Those standing upstairs could hear the elevator reach the basement level. There was a thud, a shudder and a clank. Then silence.

"What are they doing?" Egg wondered. He peered worriedly into the elevator shaft.

"I can't see a thing and I don't hear them. Do you think they're all right?" Holly wondered.

"Oh, they've got to be," Todd said. "What could go wrong?"

"Binky's not screaming," Lexi pointed out. "That's very strange."

"It is awful quiet down there, isn't it?" Todd agreed.

Holly and Lexi instinctively reached for each other's hands and moved nearer the boys.

"Jerry? Binky? Are you down there? Can you hear us?"

Silence.

"Maybe we should go get the owner," Lexi said, her voice shaky. "Why doesn't Binky *say* something? She jabbers all the time. Now, when we really want to hear her talk, she won't say boo."

They all leaned into the elevator shaft, their bodies tense, their backs rigid. Suddenly, from behind them came an ear-splitting squeal. "Boo!"

The foursome nearly pitched headfirst into the blackened shaft. Behind them, laughing, stood Binky and Jerry.

"Where did you two come from?" Egg asked indignantly.

"We just tiptoed up the stairs behind you," Binky clapped her hands with glee. "Wasn't it great? You were scared, Egg. You were really scared!"

"You're a creep, Binky McNaughton," Egg huffed, his face red with embarrassment.

"You really are, Binky. We were worried about you," Lexi said.

Binky tittered and giggled. "I gotcha that time, guys. I gotcha. I gotcha. I gotcha."

Holly was the first to laugh. "Give her a break. It was a great trick."

"You know, it *was* pretty funny," Todd admitted. "We were scared out of our wits."

Binky's eyes were still sparkling. "It was fun, wasn't it? Just like a terrific horror flick!"

"I still don't understand why you think so much about being scared, and about ghosts and horror movies."

"I told you before, Lexi, it's fun. I like it."

"It seems to me that you shouldn't think about such things," Lexi insisted. "The Bible says, 'Think about things that are true and honorable and right.'"

"Lexi, you're too serious sometimes," Binky said. "It was *fun* scaring you! It was fun *being* scared. That's why I like horror movies, because I can jump and squeal and act as crazy as I want to."

"You jump and squeal and act crazy anyway, Binky," her brother pointed out.

Lexi remembered what her mother had said about fear. There is something thrilling about being afraid, yet there comes a point at which the thrill disappears and the fear becomes real, frightening, unmanageable.

Lexi knew that when Binky entered that elevator shaft, she wasn't having fun. Of course it had been fun to sneak from the basement and scare them all, but she sensed that Binky had not been completely in control of how she felt. All this talk about spooks, ghosts and horror shows made Lexi uncomfortable. She'd rather have her mind set on honorable things as the Bible admonished.

Chapter Seven

It was Holly Agnew's first match of the tourney and she wasn't looking good.

"What's wrong with her?" Todd wondered aloud as he and Lexi stood on the sidelines. "Her serve is off. Her backhand is off. She looks like an amateur out there."

"She looks all right to me." Binky McNaughton walked up beside them. "I couldn't play tennis that well."

"But you don't have half the experience as Holly Agnew has," Todd pointed out. "She's unsteady today."

"Wouldn't *you* be if you had all these people watching you, expecting you to do something marvelous?" Binky insisted.

Most of Cedar River was out to see Holly. Fortunately, they didn't seem to mind that she wasn't playing up to her ability. A cheer went up from the crowd as Holly put away the final ball and scored a victory.

"Phew, I'm glad that's over," Todd commented. "I didn't think she'd pull that one off."

"I don't know much about tennis," Binky admitted, "but she does look nice in that outfit. Is that one of the Holly Agnew Creations that she's going to be sponsoring?"

"Holly Agnew almost lost this match and you're only concerned about her *clothes*?" Todd could not believe Binky's comment.

"I'm just trying to point out that you take this game too seriously, Todd. Lighten up."

"I'd like to, Binky, but just looking at Holly tells me that there's something wrong."

The threesome turned to watch Holly leave the court. Todd was right. The girl looked pale and shaken when she should have been invigorated by her win.

"Maybe we can catch her before she goes into the locker room," Todd suggested.

They intercepted Holly only seconds before she disappeared through the locker room door.

"Holly, wait up!" Lexi called.

Holly gave Lexi a weak smile. "Pretty rotten game, huh?"

"I thought you looked wonderful," Binky responded loyally. "And I love your outfit."

"Thanks," Holly said dully, looking at Todd. "But I know *you* could see it was a rotten game. I was really out of step, wasn't I?"

"It wasn't what I expected," Todd admitted frankly. "I've seen you look better in tournaments on television."

"That's because I've been better in other tournaments. This is the worst I've played in years." She shook her head grimly. "My game is really off today. I apologize. I'm just lucky I won."

"Aren't you feeling well?" Lexi wondered. "You look pale."

"I'm tired today. Tony made me go to bed early

last night so I'd be ready for the game today, but I didn't sleep very well. In fact, I can hardly remember sleeping at all."

"Too much excitement, I suppose," Lexi offered.

Holly shook her head. "No, that wasn't it. It was the voices."

"What do you mean, Holly?" Todd asked with obvious concern.

"Frankly, I'm not sure." Holly's eyes were dark with confusion. "I kept hearing whispering outside my walls all night."

"What were the voices saying?" Todd asked.

"I couldn't tell. Sometimes I'd get up and put my ear to the wall, but the sounds were muffled. I went out into the hallway and no one was there. I even went into the rooms on either side of mine, but they were both empty. Still, I could hear voices."

Binky, who'd been listening intently, finally spoke up. "Ghosts. It's a haunted house. You were hearing ghosts."

"I don't believe in ghosts, Binky," Holly said. "But, about 4:00 A.M., you could have talked me into it. I couldn't figure out where the voices were coming from."

"Are you sure it wasn't Tony and some of the others having a conversation downstairs?" Lexi asked.

"That's what I thought, too, until I went downstairs. No one was there. The whole house was dark and quiet, yet every time I returned to my room, I heard the voices."

"Ooooh, this is definitely strange," Binky spoke under her breath. "Supremely! The rumors are true. The Hanson house *is* haunted."

"Did you check Tony's room, Holly?" Lexi asked, trying to ignore Binky. "Are you *sure* that he and the others were asleep?"

"Well, I didn't actually go into their rooms," Holly admitted.

"Then that's it. There was someone in the house talking. The sounds of the voices were simply following the walls, coming through the air ducts. There's got to be an explanation." Todd tried to sound confident.

Holly's features relaxed. "It was silly of me. Why didn't I just go into Tony's room? I would have seen that he wasn't in bed. Then I would have been able to relax and ignore the sounds."

"Do you really think that's all it was, Lexi, voices of those in the house with Holly?"

"I'm positive, Binky. There is no such thing as a ghost—not in the Hanson house, and not haunting Holly."

"It does sound pretty far-fetched, doesn't it?" Binky's thin shoulders drooped. "But it could have been," she added sheepishly.

Holly went into the locker room then, and Binky wandered off to say hello to one of her neighbors. Lexi and Todd discussed Holly's strange story between themselves.

"What do you think's going on?" Lexi asked.

"I don't know. Something very odd is happening. Holly wouldn't make up stories about voices, or anything else that might jeopardize her tennis match. She looked exhausted today. It nearly ruined her game."

"I'm worried about her, Todd. She doesn't have

anyone here to help her except us. Her coach seems so cold and unfriendly. He isn't like family."

"We aren't her family either, Lexi."

"No, but we could be. At least we're friends. I'd like to help her but I don't know how."

"If Holly has a good night's sleep tonight and plays a solid game tomorrow, maybe this thing with the voices will be forgotten." Todd sounded hopeful.

Binky joined them again. "I have to go to the library to return some books, Lexi. Would you like to come with me?"

"Sure." Lexi waved goodbye to Todd and joined Binky at the clubhouse gate.

"The books are at home," Binky said as the two girls walked away from the tournament site. "The library doesn't open until three. I checked out some books on poltergeists and serial killers. They were really scary."

"Oh, Binky, first horror movies and now horror books," Lexi said, shaking her head.

"It gives me a thrill. Anyway, with a book, when I get scared, I can close it." Binky tossed her head. "You should be proud of me, Lexi. I'm becoming educated."

"Yeah, right. About all kinds of stupid things."

When they arrived at the McNaughton household, Egg was sitting on the front steps thumbing through the pages of a book.

"Hey, what are you doing with my books?" Binky shouted.

"I was going to take them to the library. I thought you'd forgotten."

"Oh," Binky relaxed. "That was nice of you."

"Self-preservation. Last time you checked the books out on my library card, I had to pay the fine."

Binky scooped up the books and tucked them under her arm. "Lexi's going to the library with me."

"Great idea." Egg stood up and stretched his lanky frame. "I think I will too. They're holding a book for me on the environment. I want to do a little reading about recycling plastic."

When they arrived, Binky glanced at her watch. "Good! The library opens right now." They hurried up the steps and entered the large, wood-paneled doors. To their surprise, the huge main room of the library was not silent. In fact, three librarians were standing at the desk chatting in high-pitched voices, cutting through the usual quiet like a knife.

"How come they're not whispering?" Binky wondered. "If we talked like that, we'd be in big trouble."

"Something's weird, Binky."

It took them a few moments to realize what was wrong. "Look!" Lexi exclaimed, pointing toward the shelves. "The books are backwards!" Every volume was turned spine inward on the shelves.

Egg whistled under his breath. "What do you suppose happened?"

Lexi and her friends approached the cluster of librarians as one waved a note in the air. "I've never heard the likes of this," she said indignantly. "Library ghosts, indeed."

"Ghosts?" Binky echoed.

"Oh, hello, Lexi, Binky, Egg," the librarian greeted them. Then she blushed a bright pink. "Did I say ghosts? Excuse me. I didn't mean to say that."

"You might as well tell them," one of the other

librarians said. "Perhaps they can shed some light on this."

"What happened to the books?" Egg asked.

"That's what we'd like to know!" The head librarian was obviously angry. "We arrived at 2:45 to open the building, and that's when we discovered that every volume had been turned around. This note was left on my desk." She thrust it at Lexi.

Dear Librarian:

This library has been dull as a tomb for too many years. Even ghosts get bored. If you can't find a way to liven the place up, I guess I'll have to do it myself. Keep this in mind next time you tell a library patron to be silent. Libraries should be fun. I'll be watching you. If you value your books, don't scold those who read them.

The Library Ghost.

"It's a prankster, of course," Lexi said matter-of-factly.

"A rather ambitious prankster," the librarian added. "It took a great deal of time and effort to handle all these books."

Egg wandered from behind the shelves. "It's only the books out front that are turned around," he announced.

"Thank goodness for that! I thought we'd be sorting out this mess for weeks."

"It really is a ghost," Binky announced with renewed enthusiasm. "He's everywhere. The flags. The headless statue. Holly's voices. Now this. When is someone going to believe me?"

"It's pranksters," Lexi said emphatically. "This

ghost thing is getting out of hand, Binky. You've got to admit that. Come on, let's go."

The three stepped back out into the sunlight. Lexi sat down on the top step, her elbows resting on her knees and her chin cupped in her hands. "Something has to be done. This is probably the strangest thing that's ever happened to me." Lexi rested her head against one of the big bronze lions flanking the front door of the library. "Someone thinks it's funny to be playing tricks on the people of Cedar River. We seem to be the only ones connecting these pranks."

"That's because we've been around when each one has been discovered," Egg said logically.

"You're right, Egg," Lexi acknowledged, "and that gives us added responsibility."

"What do you mean? I didn't have anything to do with these pranks!"

"I know that, Egg. But because we are aware of them all, I think we should try to find out who's playing these tricks. If we put our heads together, I'm sure we can come up with some ideas."

"No," Binky squeaked. "I think ghosts get mad at you if you interfere in their business."

"There's no such thing as a ghost, Binky."

Binky's jaw thrust out stubbornly. "I say there's a whole bunch of them. They're haunting Cedar River. One has moved into Holly's house. There's one in the park and now there's one in the library. Or maybe it's some horribly deformed creature that lives in the sewers beneath Cedar River and just comes up to torment people. Or—" Binky's imagination was running wild, "—maybe there's some sort of a swamp creature that lives in the river and doesn't want it cleaned up. Maybe we made him mad by trying to make Cedar River a nicer place and he's getting even. We wrecked his home and now he wants to wreck ours."

Egg rolled his eyes. "Oh, Binky, stuff a sock in it. I can always tell when you've been watching too many crazy movies."

"I have to agree with Egg, Binky. These are very *human* ghosts we're dealing with."

"I wish I could be so sure about that," Binky responded solemnly.

"You can be." Lexi put her hand on her friend's arm. "Binky, all this talk of spooks and ghosts doesn't scare me. Do you know why? Because my faith is in the Lord. I've got the highest power in the entire world on my side. Ghosts aren't real. God is real." Lexi could feel her friend's arm quiver.

"You're probably right, Lexi. I know I babble too much about all the movies I see. Sometimes, once I see a movie, it's stuck in my mind and I can't get it out. It gets all confused with the real world around me."

"Don't you think that's a good reason not to watch those movies, Binky?" Lexi reasoned.

"I know deep in my heart they aren't the greatest thing for me," Binky admitted. "I guess when I really think about it, I know too that these pranks are being played by human beings and not ghosts, but I'm still scared."

"What are you scared of, Binky?" Egg asked with genuine brotherly concern.

"I don't want to make whoever's doing these things angry," Binky said bluntly. "Somebody's taking a lot of time and effort to make strange things happen. What would they do to us if we got in their way?"

Binky had a valid point. Did the prankster have a plan he didn't want interrupted? Would Lexi's idea to hunt him down put them in danger?

"I don't want trouble, Binky, but these pranks are getting out of hand." Lexi's jaw was set with determination. "I think it's up to us to do something about it."

"You're probably the bravest person I know," Binky told Lexi as the three of them walked toward the Leighton home to make some telephone calls.

"I'm not so brave. I'm just not frightened of goblins and ghosts, because I know they don't exist. These are *human* troublemakers, Binky. And somehow, I'm not afraid of them either."

"I'm beginning to agree with you. But it *is* kind of fun to think about real honest-to-goodness, float-without-feet, clanking chains and haunt-in-the-night ghosts. Maybe we should leave them for the haunted mansion at the County Fair, though."

"Good idea. I'm convinced that's the only place ghosts belong."

Once they reached Lexi's house, they called Todd and Jennifer. While they were waiting for them to arrive, Egg and Binky popped popcorn while Lexi made a large pitcher of lemonade.

"What's going on?" Jennifer came through the open door with Todd close behind.

Enthusiastically and with only a few embellishments, Binky explained what had happened at the library that afternoon.

Todd whistled through his teeth. "So now there's a *library* ghost," he said. "First the flags, then the statue, and now the library. There seems to be a pattern developing here."

"What kind of a pattern?" Binky asked.

"All these pranks are taking place in public buildings or in places that are easily accessible to just about anyone. None of the pranks have been anything really harmful. My guess is that someone wants to see Cedar River stirred up for a while."

"But Cedar River is already stirred up," Jennifer pointed out. "That tennis tournament has brought more excitement to town than anything that's happened in the past year."

"That's true. Maybe someone's trying to draw attention away from the tournament."

"Why would anyone want to do that?" Binky wondered.

"The pranks are the type that teenagers would do. If we put our heads together, I'm sure we can solve the mystery." Todd glanced at his watch. "Mike wants me to close up the garage this evening, so I'd better go now."

"Jennifer, why don't you and Binky spend the night?" Lexi invited. "Todd can pick Egg up in the morning, and we should be able to wrap this mystery up over breakfast. What do you think?"

"You're a very confident detective, Lexi," Jennifer said.

Lexi dug deep into the popcorn. "Of course I'm confident. I'll be working with the greatest teenage minds in Cedar River. Did you forget?"

Jennifer tapped her forehead with her index finger. "Then we'd better get to sleep early. Otherwise, this great mind is going to be tired."

"I think that Holly is just about the prettiest girl I've ever seen," Binky announced later that evening, as the three girls prepared for bed. "Don't you?"

"She's really attractive," Lexi agreed. "And nice."

"I wish someone would say that about me."

"You're nice, Binky," Lexi protested.

"No, that I'm really attractive. I'm going to spend the rest of my life looking like somebody's little sister."

"Well you *are* somebody's little sister," Jennifer teased.

Binky ground her teeth in frustration. "Don't remind me. How would you like to go through life being Egg's little sister?"

"It's quite a challenge, but somebody's gotta do it." Jennifer grinned. "Look at it this way. Egg's not as obnoxious as he used to be."

"True, but he's still a nut."

"Nobody will argue with that," Jennifer agreed.

"I think when Egg matures, he's going to be just wonderful," Lexi said. "He'll probably invent the cure for the common cold or discover new life at the bottom of the sea. Or maybe he'll be the one who figures out how to recycle all of the plastics that are cluttering up the environment." Lexi pulled on her furry yellow bathrobe and matching slippers. "Imagine. Egg, a famous person. Maybe he'll be the President and we'll be invited to the White House."

"I appreciate the fact that you always look for the

best in everyone." Binky wore baby-doll pajamas in a lavender flower print on pink background. She looked about ten years old.

Jennifer, in a silky nightshirt and big slouch socks, sat on the corner of Lexi's bed. "I think we're all going to be famous when we grow up. Maybe I'll be a child psychologist and work with kids who have dyslexia. Or do research on how to help dyslexic kids learn more easily."

"Everybody's got these great plans." Binky sank to the edge of the bed dejectedly. "I'm just hoping to graduate from high school without much trouble."

Lexi put down her hairbrush. "I think this conversation is going nowhere. Maybe we should change the subject."

"Yes. Let's." Binky clapped her hands. "Why don't we do something fun?" She looked around the room. "Have you gotten any new tapes or CD's lately, Lexi?"

"Not a one." Lexi shook her head. "I'm saving my money for a leather jacket I saw at the mall. My folks told me if I wanted it I'd have to buy it myself."

"How about games?"

"Nah, kid stuff." Jennifer made a face. "I suppose it's too late to make fudge."

"I think so, Jennifer. We might wake Ben."

"What are we going to do?"

Binky's eyes brightened. "I know. Let's tell ghost stories! I've got a great one. It's about this couple who are out in their car late one night. A one-handed murderer escapes from the penitentiary and—"

"Let's not tell ghost stories," Lexi interrupted with exaggerated patience.

"Yeah, let's not and say we did," Jennifer added.

"You guys are no fun at all," Binky pouted.

"Here, I've got an idea." Lexi reached for the Bible that was always on her bedside stand.

"Not that," Binky complained. "There's nothing fun in that."

"There are some terrific action adventure stories in here—even romance."

"Action adventure? Romance? In the Bible?" Binky was incredulous. "I don't think so, Lexi."

"Sure there are. Let me prove it to you," Lexi said. "Haven't you heard the story of Boaz and Ruth? Or Samson and Delilah? Or Jonah? Binky McNaughton, you don't know what kind of fun and thrills you've been missing."

Binky gave Lexi a disbelieving stare. "Thrills? In the Bible? Right."

"Surely you've heard about Jonah. He was running away from God and boarded a ship. The Lord caused a huge storm on the sea that threatened to break up the ship and drown its occupants."

"Yeah. A 'Jesus and Jaws' story, right?"

Lexi smiled. "The other men in the boat decided that in order to calm the storm, they would have to throw Jonah overboard because he was running from God."

"Nice guys."

"Mmmm. And as soon as they threw Jonah overboard, the seas were calm."

"But what happened to Jonah?" Binky was becoming interested."

"Oh, he was swallowed by a big fish. He was in the belly of the fish for three days and three nights."

"This is in the *Bible*?"

Grinning, Lexi opened her Bible and began to read.

Nearly an hour later, after a spirited discussion about fish, water and men of God, the girls fell into a peaceful slumber. None of them dreamed what incredible things the next day would hold.

Chapter Eight

"More milk for your cereal, Binky?" Lexi asked. "How about another piece of toast?"

Binky shook her head and stared grimly at her bowl. "I'm not used to eating breakfast, Lexi."

"Mom won't let me out the door without breakfast. She says it gives me a good start, helps me think better."

"Maybe that's your problem, Binky," Jennifer said, spreading honey on her toast. "You should eat breakfast."

"Very funny," Binky snorted. "Cereal's OK, but there's nothing more gross in the morning than a couple of fried eggs on a plate." She shuddered. "It's like two yellow eyeballs staring at you, daring you to eat them."

"You do have a way of ruining a person's appetite, Binky."

"Ooops," Ben giggled as a spray of cereal landed in Binky's direction. "Sorry."

Jennifer burst out laughing.

"Ben, quit playing in your cereal," Lexi demanded, trying not to smile.

"It was an accident, Lexi."

"Well, it wouldn't have happened if you were eating, Ben."

Ben looked up innocently and gave them a wide smile.

"Are you people *always* this cheerful in the morning?" Binky grumbled, wiping her face with her napkin. "Everyone's grumpy at our house. Dad can't even talk until he's had his second cup of coffee."

"Mornings are the best part of the day," Lexi insisted. "A brand new chance to start over."

"Right. A brand new chance to finish all the things you didn't get done the day before—and the day before that, and the day before that . . ."

"I can see you're Miss Gloom and Doom in the morning," Jennifer observed. "What would cheer you up anyway?" Just then, the doorbell chimed.

"Company," Ben announced. "That'll cheer up Binky. Company."

Lexi peered out the window. "It's Todd and Egg. They're late." She opened the door and the two boys stepped inside.

It looked like Todd had roused Egg from a deep sleep. His hair was obviously uncombed—it stood in spikes every whichway on his head. His shirt was mis-buttoned and half his collar was tucked in. Unmatched slouch socks sagged above his untied hitops.

"Egg, you look like an unmade bed!" Binky frowned.

"Todd, is something wrong?" Lexi asked. "You look worried."

"Something is very wrong, Lexi. Holly Agnew is missing."

"Missing! No! But, how—we just saw her yesterday. Where did she go?"

Todd flung himself into one of the kitchen chairs and put his head in his hands. "The tennis committee thinks she's run away."

"Holly? But why would she run away? She had a bad game yesterday, but she still won. She was looking forward to today's matches. She felt she could do much better," Lexi reasoned.

"Her coach, Tony, is missing too," Todd went on. "The committee believes he's gone looking for her."

"What makes them think so?"

"There was a note left in his room."

"What did it say?" Lexi was becoming more and more anxious.

"I didn't see it, but everyone at the tournament headquarters was talking about it this morning. In it, Tony hinted that Holly was upset over her poor showing in the match yesterday, that she was very depressed and he was worried about her. He said she'd gone off to be by herself and he'd gone after her. He assured everyone he'd bring her back as soon as possible and not to worry. He thought the tournament should continue as scheduled. Coach Barris said things like this are common to people who have achieved too much status too quickly."

"So, they think Holly was depressed and ran away because of it?" Lexi asked.

"I guess so. The committee kept talking about the fact that she wasn't playing very well."

"But don't you think it was because of the voices she heard and her lack of sleep, Todd? She was tired. She wasn't depressed!"

"I tried to tell them that, but everyone ignored me. They all concluded she was depressed because of her game. After that, I didn't dare mention the voices. They might have thought Holly was really losing it."

"I can't believe they'd think Holly ran away because she didn't play well yesterday!"

"They were all discussing the general pressures of stardom, too, and how it probably finally got to Holly. She's been on the cover of every news magazine in the country, she's been to New York and California to film commercials, she does interviews on television and radio. The sports section of every magazine and newspaper has mentioned her at some time or other. It *is* quite a bit for a sixteen-year-old to handle."

"But, Holly is one of the least depressed people I have ever met!" Lexi exclaimed. "She was tired yesterday. You could tell. And she would never have mentioned those voices if it weren't true. It's too . . . flaky . . . a thing to make up. It would be hard on her reputation too, just like running away is. I don't think Holly would risk it."

"Maybe not, but we have to remember that we've just met Holly. We don't know what's happened in her life before this. The committee also said they think Holly may have been upset because her parents aren't at the tournament."

"But Holly said they were coming soon."

"I don't think the committee realized that. I tried to tell them, but they weren't listening to me. They were too upset."

"Well, if you ask me, they aren't listening to Holly

either. The only person they seem to believe is her coach. Holly is just a commodity to everyone else. I'm beginning to think the only people she's a real person to is us!"

"I agree with you, Lexi," Todd said. "But, what are we going to do about it? The people in charge are convinced Holly was depressed and simply ran away from it all."

"Don't forget the voices," Lexi reminded him.

"That makes me uncomfortable," Jennifer finally admitted. "I can't figure out where the voices fit into the rest of this story."

Binky snapped her fingers. "Don't you see? Here it is, the fourth mystery! First the flags, then the statue, the library ghost, and now—a missing star!" She leaned back in her chair and closed her eyes. "Ooooh, it's just too exciting for words."

"Binky," Lexi said, glaring at her, "cut it out."

Binky's eyes flew open. "Well, she is missing, isn't she? This is quite a bit more serious than the other weird things that have been happening around here."

"I think your vivid imagination is working overtime."

"No, I'm right. I know I'm right," Binky said stubbornly.

Just then the kitchen door opened and Lexi's father walked in.

Lexi was startled at the odd, tense expression on his face. "Dad, is something wrong?" She glanced at the clock on the stove. "What brings you home?"

"Oh, I was out on a house call," he explained, tossing the mail onto the counter. "I decided to come home and shower before I went back to the clinic."

"You look worried."

Mrs. Leighton entered the kitchen. "What's wrong, Jim?"

"You can't get by with anything in this family," Mr. Leighton said, shaking his head. He pulled out a chair and sank into it. "I'll take a cup of coffee. Just black, please."

Mrs. Leighton placed a steaming mug in front of him. "Now, please explain what's going on."

"There are some very strange things going on in this town, and no one seems to know why they're happening."

"Oh?" Lexi said carefully. She looked around at her friends. Binky's expression was triumphant—an "I told you so" written all over her face.

"There is a problem with the tennis tournament too," Dr. Leighton continued. "That young tennis player, Holly Agnew, is missing. Apparently she's run away."

"How awful!" Mrs. Leighton exclaimed.

"But that's not all. It seems that the pranksters who've been prowling Cedar River have gone all out this time. All the fountains in the town have turned red over night."

Binky let out a stifled scream. "Blood!" Her face turned pale. "The fountains have turned to blood!" She threw her arms around herself and rocked back and forth. "Oh, this is terrible. This is terrible. What are we going to do? What are we going to do?"

"Binky, you're freaking out. Calm down," Lexi admonished.

"I saw a movie like this," Binky said, her eyes

wide and expressionless. "All the water in the city ran red with blood. There was murder and mayhem everywhere . . ."

"The water is dyed to look like blood in the movies, Binky," Dr. Leighton assured her, patting Binky's shoulder. "The water in Cedar River hasn't turned to blood. It's been tinted with some sort of dye. The water treatment plant is working on getting the fountains cleaned up right now. By noon they should have it all taken care of."

"You're sure it wasn't blood?" Binky said suspiciously.

"Oh, Binky, don't be so gullible," Jennifer snapped. "You're so hung up on those weird movies you watch. They affect everything in your life. You're not even making sense."

"That settles it," Lexi announced. "We're going to do some sleuthing. We need to find out what's going on in this town."

"Good. You kids do that." Dr. Leighton stood up. "I'm going to take a shower."

Lexi turned to her friends. "We'll get to the bottom of this mystery no matter what it takes."

"Which mystery?" Todd asked. "The pranks or Holly's disappearance?"

"Both. But we have to find Holly first. She isn't the type to run off. It's inconsistent with her personality. I believe we're the only friends Holly has here."

"What about her coach and the people she hired to be with her?" Jennifer asked.

"Tony isn't her friend," Lexi said. "He's in this for the money."

"Well, what are we going to do first?" Binky wondered.

Egg leaned forward eagerly. "We'll have to check out the last place Holly was seen."

"That would be the Hanson house," Binky groaned. "Are you sure we want to go there?"

"There aren't any ghosts, Binky, remember?" Lexi stressed. "There may be pranksters and there may be kidnappers, but there aren't any ghosts."

"I don't think I like the sound of kidnappers any better than the sound of ghosts."

———

The Hanson house was boiling with activity and turmoil. There were cars everywhere.

"What are you kids doing here?" A stranger greeted them at the door.

"We're friends of Holly. We'd like to come in and talk to—"

"She's not here." The door slammed in their faces.

Todd turned to Binky, Egg and Jennifer, "You stay here. If anyone comes up who might listen to you, grab them. Tell them you don't think Holly's run away. Tell them about the voices. Lexi and I will go to the back and see if we can get in that way."

The two of them moved through the manicured gardens to the back of the house. Several policemen and newspaper reporters were having a heated discussion. Quietly, Todd and Lexi moved up the stairs and onto the porch. They knocked at the screen door.

"Come in," someone yelled from deep within the house. Lexi and Todd stepped inside. There were people everywhere waving their hands and talking in loud voices.

"It's a zoo here," Todd muttered. "How can anyone

discover what's happened to Holly in this kind of a circus?"

Lexi grabbed the arm of a passing gentleman. "Sir, I'd like to talk to you about Holly—"

"Sorry, I'm not talking to the press." The man escaped Lexi's grasp and moved on.

"He thought I was from the press?"

"He didn't even look at you," Todd assured Lexi. "He looked right through you."

They moved through the rooms methodically, trying to catch the eye or the ear of someone who might listen to them. "There are more people standing here arguing about what to do than there are people taking action," Todd commented. "The tennis committee can organize a tournament, but they certainly can't organize a manhunt."

"I don't think they're trying to," Lexi pointed out. "They think Holly ran away on a whim." Her eyes darkened. "I just don't believe that, Todd. Not Holly."

They were walking along the wall beneath the grand steps that led to the second floor when Lexi paused. "Stop. Wait a minute." She stood as still as a doe being stalked in the forest.

"What is it, Lexi?"

"Shhh," she put a finger to her lips. "Listen."

Todd cocked his head. "I don't hear anything."

"Stand where I am and listen."

"I don't hear anything . . . wait, what's that?"

"I'm sure, absolutely positive that I heard voices just now. Voices coming out of that wall."

"There are probably voices coming from the light fixtures today," Todd joked.

Lexi moved to the wall and put her ear against

the wooden panel. "I *do* hear something, Todd."

"What're they saying?"

"I can't tell. It's very muffled—a thumping sound and a groaning, too." Lexi's eyes widened. "Come and listen again, please."

Todd stepped closer to the paneling again. "You're right. I hear voices too. But they're not coming from behind this panel. They're coming from somewhere else in the house."

"The secret passage?"

Todd nodded briskly. "It makes sense. The passage probably leads through the house. Someone is talking somewhere else and we're hearing the faint sound of their voices down here."

Todd spun around as a young policeman walked by them in the hallway. "Help, sir. You've got to help us. Please. You have to listen to us."

The policeman frowned and was about to brush Todd off when a light of recognition lit his eyes. "Say, aren't you a Winston kid? I went to school with your brother Mike. My name's Evan Cramer."

Todd sagged against the wall in relief. "Great! I'm Todd. And this is my friend, Lexi Leighton. Evan, we have to talk to you about something. We think we have a clue in the disappearance of Holly Agnew."

Officer Cramer's expression turned professional again. "Talk fast, then. We've got some pretty worried people here."

"Listen to this wall," Todd pointed toward the wood paneling.

Evan gave him a doubtful look. "Listen to the wall?"

"Yes. Just listen, please."

The policeman walked over and leaned against the paneling. His eyes began to widen. "There's somebody in there!"

"Let us explain. We were visiting Holly here yesterday. She showed us a secret passageway she'd discovered in her bedroom. We think someone's in the passage and we're hearing the echo of their voices in the wall."

"The Chief has got to hear this," Cramer said as he directed Lexi and Todd into the large living room. "Why didn't you tell anyone before?"

Todd groaned. "We've been trying to. No one would pay any attention to us."

Soon Todd and Lexi were the center of attention in the room. The Chief of Police listened intently as they told their story of Holly's personality as they perceived it, and about the voices that she claimed kept her awake at night. His expression was doubtful until the young policeman corroborated their evidence.

"Well, youngsters, maybe we'd better take a look at this secret passageway you're talking about."

Lexi led the way as the chief, Cramer, and Todd followed her upstairs. It took a few seconds for her to locate the fake book that concealed the opening to the hidden passage.

With a swift pull on the volume, the shelf swung open. Everyone stood in shocked amazement as they discovered Holly's coach, Anatoli Weare, huddled on the small landing inside the secret passage. He was bound and gagged.

"Tony!" Todd and Lexi gasped in unison.

Suddenly, the Cedar River Police Chief started

giving orders. "Untie him. Get him up here. Hurry. Somebody call an ambulance."

Evan Cramer pulled Tony out of the opening, removed the gag and deftly cut away the ropes that bound his hands and feet. For a moment, Tony was speechless. He coughed and sputtered and wiped his mouth with the back of his hand.

"What took you so long? I've been scratching and tapping on the walls all night, trying to get someone to find me in here."

"Well, you might have been sitting here all week if it weren't for these two." The Police Chief looked with reluctant admiration at Lexi and Todd. "They're the ones who heard you."

"Where's Holly?" Tony's voice crackled with anxiety. "Is she all right?"

"We were hoping you'd know," the Police Chief answered bluntly.

"I've been tied up in that hole all night. Holly and I were together in the living room when someone came through the French doors. I didn't have a chance to turn around before I was hit on the head."

"So you have no idea what's happened to Holly?"

Tony rubbed his head. "Frankly, I don't even know what happened to me."

"May I look at this, sir?" Evan Cramer tugged on an envelope that was tucked in Tony's breast pocket. Before Tony could answer, he opened it. "It looks like a ransom note for Holly Agnew."

"What?" Tony's jaw dropped.

"It's written in the same hand as the note we found in Tony's bedroom," Officer Cramer announced.

"What note? I didn't leave any note in my bedroom," Tony sputtered.

"There was a note found saying that Holly was depressed and that she'd run away. It also said you'd followed her."

Tony was dumbfounded. "That's ridiculous! Holly wasn't the least bit depressed. One bad game wouldn't get a girl like Holly down."

"Well, now it appears that instead of a runaway, we have a kidnapping on our hands. Whoever knocked you out and took Holly knew that it would be a long time before you'd be found in that secret passage. They left the letter in your room as a red herring to put us off the track." The Police Chief glanced at the ransom note and whistled. "They're asking for a very large sum of money for Holly's return."

"How much?" Officer Cramer wondered. When the Police Chief showed him the figure, Evan's eyes told everyone it was a large sum indeed.

"Well, whoever asked for this was probably hiding in the passageway waiting for the right opportunity," the Police Chief concluded.

"Those were the voices Holly heard at night!" Lexi exclaimed.

"So the kidnappers spent the night in the house with Holly and when the time was right, when Tony and Holly were alone, they took her." The Cedar River Police Chief turned to Todd and Lexi. "I'm not quite sure who you kids are, but you have to be commended for your quick thinking and your diligence. Now, is there anything else you know?"

They both shook their heads somberly. Lexi had

a sinking feeling in the pit of her stomach. She watched the medics examine Tony's head. It was one thing to be an amateur detective trying to discover who a prankster might be, it was quite another to have a kidnapping to solve and a real mystery on their hands.

Chapter Nine

Egg flung himself across a park bench with a moan as Todd and Lexi finished telling their friends what had happened at the Hanson house. "This is serious, guys," he stated. "This isn't kid stuff. Maybe we should leave finding Holly Agnew to the police."

"We have to do that," Lexi agreed. "But perhaps we can help them in some way. After all, they wouldn't have found Tony in the secret passage if it hadn't been for us."

"I don't think we're that smart," Binky said. "I think Holly's lost forever."

"Stop it, Binky. We *are* going to find her. We can help," Jennifer said.

"I agree," Todd said. "We have a different perspective on things than the police or even other adults do. We think like Holly. We're her age, and we're the only ones in town who've had an opportunity to get to know her. It's a good idea for us to put our heads together to see what we come up with."

"Won't it be dangerous?" Binky asked. "Kidnappers are dangerous people, aren't they?"

Egg hooted from the bench. "Is that my sister talking? The one who loves movies with ax murderers and chainsaw killers? The one who says you can't have a thrill without some danger?"

"That's in the movies, Egg. This is real life."

"My point exactly. You live in a fantasy world in the movies, Binky. In real life, when the dangers affect you, you see that it's not so fun after all, that it's serious business and people could get hurt."

"I really never thought about it like that before. I guess movies do make me think less about how people really feel, about real emotions." Binky was quiet for a moment. "I'm scared—for myself, but especially for Holly. Maybe we should just stick to solving the other mysteries—the library ghost and the red water in the fountains—and leave Holly's kidnapping to the police."

"First we have to ask ourselves if the kidnapping has anything to do with what else has been happening in Cedar River," Todd reminded her.

"Why would the kidnappers bother to turn the water red in the fountains?" Jennifer wondered.

"Or turn the library books upside down?" Egg added.

"Or the flags. What does that have to do with anything?" Binky concluded.

"This is all so confusing." Lexi scratched her head. "How do we know where to begin?"

"Let's start by walking around the park. Maybe somebody left a clue," Egg offered.

To get started, they all headed toward the founder's statue. "There have been so many people by the park to see this beheaded wonder, any clues were destroyed long ago," Lexi reasoned.

They stopped short at the base of the statue. The

memorial to the founder of Cedar River was whole again. His head was where it should have been, and a casual passerby would not have been able to tell that it had been broken off just a few days ago.

"It won't be so easy to behead H. T. again," Egg commented. "I hear the park maintenance welded his head to his neck this time."

"You mean it was loose before?" Lexi asked.

"Oh sure, didn't you know that? When the statue was erected, there was a big hubbub about the fact that it wasn't one solid piece of bronze. The head was separate."

"Then the pranksters already knew that the head could be easily removed, without really hurting anything," Lexi said.

"I suppose that's true, but why bother?" Todd returned.

"To cause some excitement!" Lexi concluded. "And it did, didn't it?"

"That means whoever took the head off the statue has probably lived in Cedar River eight years or more," Egg explained. "That's when the statue was installed."

"We're talking local people then, not strangers or someone from the outside," Todd added.

"It wouldn't have been anyone coming to town for the tennis tournament then," Jennifer pointed out.

"I think we're on the right track, guys," Lexi enthused. "Maybe we should go to the library next."

They all piled into Todd's car and headed for the city library. The trip was not as productive as the one to the park, though.

After a quick perusal they all stepped outside

again where they could talk about their findings. Binky looked discouraged. "I couldn't think of any good ideas in there."

Egg snorted. "Is this something new, Binky?

Before they could start one of their sibling fights, Todd stepped in. "I thought of something. Did anyone notice how many shelves of books there were?"

"It's a library, Todd!" Egg snapped.

"Yes, but it took a lot of manpower to turn all those books around."

"Manpower? You mean more than one prankster?" Binky asked.

"I'd say several. Two or three at least."

"Good point!" Lexi smiled. "We're beginning to build a profile of the troublemakers. There's more than one. There could be as many as three or four. At least one of them has lived in Cedar River eight years or more. They have to be connected in some way. Friends, probably."

"Oh, terrific," Binky groaned. "How may groups of four people or more are friends and have lived in Cedar River at least eight years?"

"Hundreds," Todd admitted.

"Too bad we don't have computer information like they have at the police station," Egg said. "Then we could run a check on all the people who have lived in Cedar River for eight years or more and come up with a list."

"But we don't have a computer, Egg, and we don't have a list. All we have is our brains," Binky said, pointing to her head.

"Well, at least I have mine, Binky. I'm not so sure about yours."

"All right, break it up you two. We need everybody pulling together on this one," Todd said, refusing to allow Binky and Egg to get into one of their spats.

"Local people. Friends. Troublemakers. Who does that describe?" It was as though a light bulb went on in Egg's skull. "Come on, you guys. I've got an idea." He ambled toward Todd's car and slid behind the wheel. "Mind if I drive, Todd?"

Todd nodded and the others scrambled into the car. It was Lexi who recognized their destination first. "Minda Hannaford's house! What are we doing here?"

Egg pulled into the alley behind the house and jumped out. "Come on." He hurried toward the garbage cans behind the garage and lifted the first lid. He stuck his head inside, and soon the gang could hear the rustling of paper and cans.

"What are you doing?" Binky demanded. "Egg, this isn't the time to recycle! We have a mystery to solve. Can't it wait?"

Egg didn't respond. He slapped the lid back on the can and lifted the lid of another. Wordlessly, he dug through each receptacle until he found what he was looking for. Finally he stood up, a large bottle in his hand and a triumphant smile on his face. "Ah-ha!" The bottle contained a residue of dark red liquid. "I've discovered one of our ghosts. This is a commercial-size bottle of food dye." Egg held it out for Binky to read the label.

"That's what was found in the fountains?" Binky asked, wide-eyed.

"I can't imagine any other reason why Minda

Hannaford would have empty bottles of food dye in her garbage."

"Where did she get it?"

"Tressa Williams," Todd blurted. "Her mother is a caterer. It wouldn't be hard for her to get something like that, would it?"

Suddenly things were beginning to make sense. "You mean the Hi-Fives are the pranksters?" Lexi gasped.

"I'm not sure if they're the library ghosts, but they're certainly the ones who turned the fountains of Cedar River blood red."

"Before we tell anyone else about this, I think we should confront Minda," Lexi said, her jaw set with determination. "This is serious. If the Hi-Fives did this, they've upset a lot of people in Cedar River."

"Minda came by the garage early this morning to pick up a spare tire that was being fixed," Todd offered. "She said the Hi-Fives were having a meeting over at Tressa's house today."

"So they'll all be together in one place. Terrific! Let's go talk to them." Lexi stomped toward the car. She could feel the adrenalin pumping through her veins. The Hi-Fives had pulled a lot of stupid stunts in the time she'd known them, but this was the biggest and the most far-reaching.

During the drive to Tressa's, Binky began to have second thoughts. "Oooh, I don't know if I want to go along with this," she moaned. "I don't want those girls mad at me. There's no telling what they might do for revenge."

"Binky McNaughton, I thought you were the brave one. You're the one who loves the horror stuff," Jennifer told her.

"Oh, let's quit bringing up those stupid movies. I'm sorry I ever started watching them." Binky flung herself against the seat and crossed her arms over her chest. "I'm not as brave as I thought I was. I don't like being scared as much as I thought I did, all right?"

"Here we are," Todd announced as he pulled up in front of the Williams' home. The front door was open, and Lexi could see several of the Hi-Fives sitting on the living room floor.

"Come on, gang. Here we go." Lexi turned toward her friends, "Egg, bring the bottles along for proof."

Tressa came to the door. "What are you guys doing here?" Her voice was anything but friendly.

"We've come to talk to the Hi-Fives," Todd announced.

"Sorry. We didn't put you on the program," Tressa retorted.

"Well, you can put us on now," Lexi said. "We have something important that we need to discuss."

Tressa turned to speak to the girls in the room. "We have company. Lexi and Todd and their *weird* friends have come to visit." Tressa opened the screen door and reluctantly allowed them inside. The girls were sprawled on the floor, the couch and the chairs. Minda was sitting at a table presiding over the group like a queen.

"We don't like to be interrupted when we're having a meeting," she said indignantly.

"Well, we don't really *like* being here," Lexi retorted.

"Then why are you here? Curiosity get the best of you? You did have a chance to be one of us, Lexi," Minda reminded her.

"At the moment, I'm awfully glad I'm not a Hi-Five."

Minda's expression darkened. "And what is that supposed to mean?"

"Show her, Egg."

With a flourish, Egg pulled two of the empty bottles from beneath his shirt. Minda stared at them in shock. The other girls in the room shifted nervously as they stared at the tell-tale bottles.

"Where did you get those?" Tressa demanded. Minda's face had gone white.

"I think you already know the answer to that, don't you?" One by one, heads began to droop.

"I can have you arrested for breaking and entering," Minda said angrily, pointing a finger at Egg.

"Breaking and entering your garbage?" Egg shot back. "Hardly. Especially considering what I found. I think your parents would be interested in knowing about this."

"Don't you dare tell my parents! We were just having a little fun."

"Fun? You've caused a lot of work for a lot of people. The city has had to empty the water from all the fountains, clean them and start them up again."

"Water's cheap," Tressa pointed out.

"Maybe, but labor isn't," Todd put in. "You girls should be ashamed of yourselves."

"I suppose you're the ones who took the head off the statue, too!" Binky blurted.

Somebody at the back of the room giggled nervously.

"And I have a hunch we've found the library ghost as well," Lexi added. "The librarians will hardly let teenagers in the door now, they're so suspicious. It took them a long time to turn those books around and put them back in the right order. It's a whole lot easier to mess things up than to clean them up, you know."

Even Minda had the grace to look a little ashamed.

"And the flags—"

"Turning the flags upside down didn't hurt anybody," Minda protested. "What's with you guys today, anyway? Since when can't some kids play a few pranks? This is a dumb, boring town. We decided to liven it up a little bit. It worked, didn't it?"

"I think you livened it up a little too much," Lexi warned. "You could be in big trouble because of it."

"You're just trying to scare us," Minda taunted. "Well, you can't. Nobody really cares what direction the flags in Cedar River are flying."

"The problem runs a little deeper than that, Minda. A lot of strange things have been happening in Cedar River. When you're involved in one of them, you might be accused of all of them."

"What is that supposed to mean?" Minda said, her eyes narrowed, her pretty face in a scowl.

"You haven't heard about Holly Agnew?"

"Holly Agnew? That boring tennis star? Who wants to hear anything about her?"

"She's been kidnapped," Lexi said evenly.

Suddenly the room was silent.

"Kidnapped?" Minda echoed.

"That's right. She turned up missing and this morning they discovered that she's been kidnapped. Her coach was found tied up in the Hanson house with a ransom note stuck in his pocket."

"We didn't have anything to do with that!" one of the girls piped. "We don't even *know* Holly Agnew. We were just trying to have a little fun."

"Minda, you're the one who said Holly Agnew shouldn't be getting all that attention," Gina Williams confessed. "It was you who suggested that we pull these pranks to take some of the attention away from her."

"I didn't want to see her hurt," Minda argued, a quiver in her voice. "Just because I didn't think she should be getting all the attention in town doesn't mean I wanted her kidnapped!"

"So you were jealous of the attention Holly was getting?" Lexi asked. "It makes sense. The pranks were your way of distracting attention from her."

"We didn't hurt anyone," Tressa pointed out. She looked pale and a little frightened. "We made sure everything we did wouldn't do any real damage. My mom uses that food dye in punch bowls all the time. And we never dreamed someone would kidnap Holly! The pranks were supposed to be innocent fun. But now, if Holly gets hurt . . . the pranks don't seem funny anymore."

"Tressa is right," Todd agreed. "The pranks were harmless enough. They didn't do anything that couldn't be easily remedied."

"Are you going to report us to the police?" came a small voice from the back of the room.

Lexi was very glad she was not a member of the Hi-Fives at that moment. "Are we going to tell on you? No, I don't think so." A corporate sigh of relief spread over room. Then Lexi continued. "You're going to be telling on yourselves."

Minda looked aghast. "What do you mean by that?"

"We'd feel rotten if we had to go to the police and tell them we'd discovered who played all the pranks," Todd said. "But, I think it would be good if you girls got together and admitted what you've done."

"You mean, *we* have to go to the police?" Tressa looked really frightened now.

"Yes. I think you should go to the library and to the Park Board and admit what you've done. The people there will have to decide what kind of punishment you deserve."

"Punishment?" one of the girls whimpered.

"Actually, I think it'll be better for you if you admit what you've done. If we turned you in, things would be a lot worse for you. This way, at least you will have learned your lesson." Todd looked around the room. "I hope."

For once, none of the Hi-Fives appeared snobbish or even self-assured. Lexi felt a twinge of sympathy for all of them. The pranks had not been worth it.

"We don't want to be connected with Holly Agnew's kidnapping," Gina said, her voice trembling.

"That's why you should go to the library and the Park Board right away."

Tressa's face was white and her eyes were filled with tears.

Even Minda looked humbled. "I think they're right. We'd better go 'fess up to what we've done before any more time passes. We don't want to be connected in any way to this kidnapping."

Minda was obviously scared, but willing to do the

right thing. Lexi was thankful she and her friends would not have to report the Hi-Fives' activities. It was a quiet, humble group that filed out of Tressa Williams' house. The girls all climbed into Tressa's van while Lexi's gang got into Todd's '49 Ford Coupe.

"Are you going to follow them?" Binky wondered.

Todd turned his car in the other direction. "Our being around would just embarrass them further."

A big whooping hooting laugh came from the backseat. "Wow!" Egg shouted. "That was some moment. You and Lexi really told them off, Todd."

"Did we?" Lexi asked. "I didn't really notice."

"We solved the mystery! And we proved that Cedar River isn't haunted." Egg gave Binky a sharp glance.

"It might not be haunted," Binky agreed, "but Holly is still missing."

A concerned silence descended over the group. Binky was right. One mystery had been solved, but the larger, more important one remained unanswered.

Chapter Ten

It was early afternoon the next day when the gang gathered at Lexi's house again to discuss Holly Agnew's disappearance. Egg was carrying a notebook of plans, sketches and ideas for solving the mystery. Binky looked a shade disappointed about the entire situation.

"What's wrong with you today?" Jennifer asked Binky. "You look as though you've lost your best friend."

"Oh, it's nothing," she said, her voice wistful. "It just seems to me that this whole thing would be easier if there *were* such things as ghosts."

"Binky McNaughton, what a crazy thing to say!"

"Well, it's true. I've always hoped there *were* ghosts, because they're so mysterious. A kidnapping is downright scary."

"The best we can do is to get ourselves organized and make some plans for finding Holly." Todd was sprawled across the Leighton's couch, his expression thoughtful. "We know that the police and the FBI are out looking for her. They can do a much better job than we can."

"Then what are we trying to do?" Binky looked confused.

"Look for Holly in places the police wouldn't think of."

His comment got everyone's attention. "What do you mean, Todd? What places?"

"Teenage places," Todd said with a laugh. "Places where kids go."

"But her kidnapper's probably an adult."

"True, but the FBI and the police would have covered all the obvious areas. We have to look at this from a new angle. It's the only hope we have."

"It's worth a shot," Egg agreed.

"Where do we start?" Lexi wondered.

"How about the school?" Todd suggested.

"Abandoned farm sites near town where kids have parties," Egg threw in.

Jennifer's face turned pink. "All those good parking spots I keep hearing about but never get to."

As the gang threw ideas back and forth, something nagged at Lexi, an unformed idea prodded at her consciousness. There was something . . . something . . . a clue of some kind, yet she couldn't put her finger on it. What would she know about Holly Agnew or her kidnapper? There was a puzzle piece missing and Lexi couldn't find it.

"Why don't we drive to the school for starters?" Todd said.

Anxious to get on the trail of the kidnapper, everyone climbed into Todd's car again and they were off to the high school.

Everything was locked up tight for the summer. The shades were drawn and every door had a chain across it.

Binky peered through the glass doors. "I don't

think the kidnapper would bring her here. It's as tight as a drum. You'd either need a janitor's key or a hacksaw."

"You're right, Binky. Bad idea." Todd looked discouraged. "Now what?"

"Let's drive around the countryside," Egg suggested. "Maybe we'll get some ideas. We can brainstorm in the car."

After nearly two hours of driving, Jennifer announced, "We aren't getting anywhere doing this. There are umpteen roads around Cedar River. We don't even know what we're looking for."

"We're never going to find her," Binky wailed. "She's probably laying dead somewhere and we've missed her entirely."

"Binky, stuff a sock in it," Egg said. "We're all worried about Holly. We don't need you spreading gloom on top of the whole situation."

For once, Binky seemed to listen to her brother. She withdrew into a shell of worried silence.

"It's going to be dark in a few hours," Todd said, looking at the sky. "Jennifer's right. We could drive around forever and not get anywhere out here."

They were all silent on the return trip to town. Lexi had a tight knot of despair in her stomach. They'd been foolish to think they could discover Holly Agnew's whereabouts.

Still, Lexi had been the one to help find Tony, Holly's coach. If only she could put her finger on the thought that was floating around in her mind, the notion that she had a vague clue about Holly's kidnapper. Lexi shook her head. This nagging thought that she had a hint to Holly's whereabouts was driving her crazy.

"Now *there's* a place no one would think to look," Binky chirped.

Everyone's head whirled in the direction in which Binky was pointing, and Todd slowed the car to a crawl. On the far side of the road they could barely make out the small country graveyard in the gathering darkness. It looked old and poorly cared for. Grave markers were tipped at odd angles, reminding Lexi of a mouth full of broken and twisted teeth. Tall grass covered most of the graves. A few had been cleared, and bore bunches of artificial flowers sprouting from metal urns.

"I'm sorry, Binky, but no one wants to look in a graveyard. That place is creepy." Egg folded his arms across his chest and sighed, as if his sister's suggestion was too bizarre to consider.

"Binky might have a good idea," Todd said.

"Huh?" Egg bolted forward.

"Usually cemeteries have toolsheds for storing gardening equipment," Todd explained. "That wouldn't be such a bad place to hide someone, at least temporarily."

"Should we take a look?" Lexi asked cautiously.

Todd pulled off the road.

"Where are the families of all these people?" Binky wondered. "Why don't they take care of these graves?"

"The families are probably long gone, too," Jennifer pointed out. "Sad, isn't it?"

"Oh, this is so irritating!" Lexi bumped the heel of her hand against her forehead in frustration.

"What's wrong with you, Lexi?" Jennifer puzzled.

"I have this feeling that I've seen or heard something important to this mystery—a clue of some sort. I should know where Holly is. I can't explain it. It's just a feeling."

"Now you're beginning to sound like me and the ghosts," Binky whimpered. She looked around the property as butterflies formed in her stomach. "Of course, it's pretty easy to think about ghosts in a place like this."

"Don't get started, Binky," Egg cautioned. "We don't need your ghost-talk now."

Nightfall was creeping in, and the damp evening air closed in around them. The branches of a barren tree rubbed its gnarled wooden fingers along the toolshed at the far end of the graveyard.

"Ooooh, I don't like that noise," Binky said with a shudder. "It sounds like a skeleton scratching another skeleton's back."

"Great. Just great. That's exactly what we needed to hear. Skeleton talk." Egg looked worried. "I think we better stick together. This place is pretty spooky." He reached for Binky's hand and, for once, she gave it to him willingly.

Todd slipped his arm around Lexi's shoulders. "It *is* a little creepy here, isn't it?"

The eerie hoot of an owl made Lexi jump. "More than a little. At night every unfamiliar sound is magnified."

Suddenly, a piercing scream rent the air and a figure came flying into their path. Flailing hands grabbed at Binky's throat. Her own scream was so high-pitched it could have shattered glass.

Egg gave a terrified roar and dropped to his knees.

"Whoa, whoa, whoa! I really scared you!" Jennifer shouted with glee. "I knocked Eggo right off his feet! Did you see the look on Binky's face? Hey, Binky, you're as white as typing paper."

"Oh . . . oh . . . you . . . you really . . . scared me!" Binky clutched her chest and rocked back and forth. "I think I'm going to have a heart attack. I think Egg *did* have a heart attack."

"Oh, be quiet, Binky," Egg said, embarrassed by his reaction to Jennifer's prank. "She tripped me, that's all."

"I did *not* trip you, Egg McNaughton!" Jennifer giggled. "I scared you."

"You did a great job, too," Lexi admitted. "My heart is beating double-time. I'm not sure the color is going to come back into Binky's cheeks until we get out of here."

"She's the one with the vivid imagination. Aren't you sorry for all the horror movies you've watched?" Jennifer asked.

Binky nodded. "I thought it was that creature that keeps popping up in all those sequels. The one with the long hair and blood on his fangs."

"Gross, Binky. That's make-believe anyway," Lexi reminded her.

"Oh, yeah." Binky glanced around. "But out here it's kind of hard to remember."

As they drew closer to the toolshed, the bony fingers of the barren tree branch scraped more loudly on the side of the shed.

"I don't like this," Binky cooed softly. "I saw a movie where some kids opened an old vault and let out all sorts of spirits and ghosts."

"Binky, that's the movies. We're in a little country graveyard within three miles of Cedar River's city limits." Todd's voice was firm and comforting. "You're letting your imagination run away with you. Nothing's going to happen here. You're scaring yourself. Can't you see that?"

"Yeah, Bink, I'm really sorry," Jennifer said apologetically. "I didn't know you'd get so shook or I wouldn't have jumped out at you. You watch too many creepy movies."

"I'm quitting," Binky said, dramatically placing her hands across her chest. "As of this minute, no more of them. My heart can't take it."

"Let's look inside this thing." Todd kicked at the door of the toolshed. Inside they heard the skitter of small rodent feet.

Binky's and Egg's eyes were round as moons.

"Here goes," Todd said with mock cheerfulness. He put his hand on the doorknob and pulled. With a wrenching creak, the door popped open.

Before any of them had time to gather their wits, there was a flutter of wings. Two black bats darted out the door, sailing low, right over Binky's head. "Augh!" A gargling sound caught in Egg's throat.

"Ick! Did you see that? Bats!" Jennifer shuddered. "They are *so* gross. I heard once that if a bat got tangled up in your hair, you'd have to cut it out because of their spiky little wings. Do you think that's true, Binky?"

Lexi turned to her friend. "Binky? Binky?"

Binky had fainted dead away.

Todd, who'd already entered the shed, came out dusting the cobwebs from his hair. "It's empty in

there. You can tell it's been home to a few night crea-
tures, nothing else. What happened?"

"Binky fainted when those bats flew out over her
head," Jennifer told him. "Help us revive her."

Lexi slapped gently at Binky's cheeks while Egg
hovered over his sister. "We need some water to
splash on her face."

Todd suddenly took charge. "Egg, shut the
toolshed door. I'll carry Binky to the car." He scooped
her up as if she were a basket of feathers. Lexi and
Jennifer followed, whispering worriedly about their
friend.

By the time they reached the Coupe, Binky was
beginning to groan and squirm in Todd's arms. Her
hands fluttered to the top of her head. "Get them
away from me."

"The bats are gone, Binky," Todd said calmly.
"They flew right over your head and into the trees.
There's nothing to be afraid of. We're going home
now."

"Home?" Her eyes fluttered opened. "I want to go
home. I never ever want to watch another horror
movie again."

Todd settled her on the front seat of his car. "I
think that's a terrific idea, Binky. You've given yourself a bad scare."

"No more horror movies. No more monster movies. No more scares," Binky chanted in a weak voice.
"I used to think it was fun to be scared at the movies,
but when you're scared in real life, it's no fun at all.
I hate it."

Todd dropped the McNaughtons off at their
house, but not before extracting a promise from Egg

that he would take care of his sister.

"How come nobody ever worries like this about me?" Egg pouted. Lexi patted his hand. "If you'd fainted, Egg, we would have fussed over you in the same way."

"Oh. So that's what it takes," Egg said grumpily, but he put his arm around his sister's shoulders. "Well, I'll take care of her, even if it is her own fault she scared herself silly."

After he'd taken Jennifer home, Todd drove Lexi to her house. "Well, that wasn't a very productive day," he sighed. "I wish we had more to show for it than one fainted girl."

"Who knows?" Lexi said wearily. "Maybe this will teach Binky not to watch those awful movies anymore. But I do feel as if we should have found a clue to Holly's whereabouts. I have this feeling that I know something that I can't put my finger on."

"You've been reading too many detective stories," Todd said with a laugh.

"Or maybe I just want so desperately to find Holly that my mind is playing tricks on me." Lexi slumped against the seat of the car. "Todd, I'm so discouraged. What must Holly be going through? Somebody's got to find her!"

"There are a lot of people looking, Lexi. We won't give up. Just because we had a bad day today doesn't mean we'll forget about Holly."

"I certainly haven't seen much of you today," Mrs. Leighton said from the kitchen as Lexi entered the house. She was removing the last of a batch of chocolate chip cookies from the pan.

"Well, it wasn't a very good day, I can tell you that."

"Still worried about your friend Holly?" Mrs. Leighton said sympathetically.

"Terribly. We went looking for her." In breathless spurts, Lexi explained what she and her friends had been doing.

"I really don't think it's wise for you young people to get involved in this, Lexi. Let the police handle it. They're experts."

"I know, Mom. It's just that I feel I should know something that would help discover Holly's whereabouts."

"Too many detective stories," Mrs. Leighton said with a smile.

"That's what Todd said." Lexi reached for a chocolate chip cookie and enjoyed its warm goodness. "We're lousy detectives. It's not as easy to be a detective as I thought it would be. The clues aren't right out there for the taking."

"Very little of life is like what you see on television or in the movies. Those are merely idealized pictures of life. People wouldn't spend money to watch movies of ordinary everyday life." Mrs. Leighton laughed lightly. "Would anyone be interested in my day, for instance—doing laundry, cleaning bathrooms, cooking supper and baking cookies? It wouldn't make much of a two-hour movie, would it."

"I don't know," Lexi said playfully. "These cookies are pretty good."

"Do you want some milk with that?" Mrs. Leighton asked.

"No, I don't think so," she sighed. "I'm really not very hungry. I keep feeling like I should be able to do something for Holly. It scares me, Mom."

"Frankly, honey, the best thing you can do for Holly right now is pray for her. God has His hand on her no matter where she is or who she's with."

God has His hand on Holly no matter where she is. The thought was comforting.

Lexi mounted the stairs to her bedroom. Before getting into bed, she fell to her knees and bowed her head. "Dear Lord," she prayed. "I'm so worried about my friend, Holly. Some evil people have kidnapped her and she's frightened and alone. Keep her from harm. I also pray for the people who are looking for her. Please let her be found soon, safe and sound." For a long time after Lexi crawled into bed, she lay awake, thinking of Holly, wondering where she might be.

The bedside clock read 2:00 A.M. when Lexi sat bolt upright. "I've got it!" she announced to the darkness. "I've got it!" An image had come into her mind with perfect clarity. "That's it," Lexi said aloud. "Now I know what's happened to Holly!"

Chapter Eleven

Lexi hurried through her breakfast so quickly that her brother Ben stared at her. "Oink, oink," Ben giggled as Lexi spooned the last of her cereal into her mouth. "Lexi eats fast."

"Sorry about that, Ben. I've got lots to do today." She pushed away from the table. "You'll have to excuse me. I have to make some telephone calls." Lexi escaped to the living room where she called each of her friends and told them to hurry to her house. She paced back and forth on the front porch until they arrived.

Jennifer came jogging down the street at the same time Todd pulled up in his '49 Ford Coupe with Egg and Binky in tow.

"What's going on?" Jennifer called.

"Yeah, what's up?" Todd asked.

"Why'd you call so early, Lexi? Did something happen?" Binky wondered.

Lexi beamed happily at her friends. "How are you feeling, Binky?" she asked.

"Much better."

"What's going on?" they all demanded.

Lexi turned to them with a huge smile. "I think I know where Holly is."

Binky and Egg groaned simultaneously. "Not an-other graveyard trip," Binky wailed. "I can't take it."

"You called us over here for that? Come on, Lexi," Jennifer said. "We looked all day yesterday and didn't have a clue. What did a good night's sleep do to make a difference?"

"You'd better explain yourself, Lexi," Todd said.

"Don't you remember? I said several times yes-terday that I thought I had a clue, that I knew some-thing that should help, but I just couldn't put my finger on it. Well, last night about 2:00 A.M., it came to me!"

"What! Tell us!" Binky chirped.

"Do you remember Holly commenting about an old blue car that seemed to turn up everywhere?"

"Oh, yeah," Jennifer remembered. "She said there must be lots of cars like that in Cedar River because she'd noticed them everywhere. Even Todd's car reminded her of it."

"Exactly. She pointed the car out to me. It was a newer model than Todd's, about the same color, but not in very good condition."

"So? What's the big deal?" Binky wondered.

"Well, the car that Holly showed me was in front of the mansion that day." She paused. "*And, it was still in front of the mansion after she was kidnapped!*"

"So?" Todd said. "That's not much of a clue, Lexi."

"Well, I'm sure the car is somehow connected to the kidnapping."

"How do you know it doesn't belong to one of the neighbors up there?" Egg asked.

"Because there aren't many neighbors, for one thing. And everyone has a long driveway. Very few people park on the street in that area."

Lexi's friends were getting frustrated.

Lexi went on, "Everywhere Holly went, she noticed that car. It seems to me that whoever was driving it was *following* Holly. I'm *sure* it's connected to the kidnappers. Holly didn't recognize the car. It didn't belong to any of her group. Whoever was driving it wanted to stay near the house."

"OK, once she was kidnapped, why would the car still be there?" Jennifer asked.

"Don't you see?" Lexi drew a breath before making her startling announcement. "I think Holly is still inside the house!"

"What?"

"You're kidding."

"Why else would the car that followed her around still be at the house?" Lexi asked.

"Maybe it's an old junker that was abandoned," Egg reasoned. "Or maybe it ran out of gas."

"It's the perfect plan. The house is the one place the police and the FBI would never suspect. They might dust it for fingerprints, but once they found the ransom note, they wouldn't have cause to be tearing out the walls to find her. Why not kidnap Holly Agnew and keep her in the very house she'd been living in?"

"It doesn't make sense, Lexi," Binky said.

"What about the secret passageway?"

"Of course, but that's where Holly's coach was found," Jennifer reminded her.

"Well, if there is one secret passage in the house, why can't there be two? Holly could be kidnapped without ever being taken from the house! It'd be easy to return her once the ransom money was collected."

Everyone was quiet, thinking.

"You know, Lexi's got a point," Todd finally agreed. "A little crazy, but a possibility. That old house could be filled with secret passages. We never did figure out where those voices Holly heard were coming from. There could be an entire room sealed off in that house."

"Binky's dad says the people who lived there were nutty as fruitcakes. That means the secret passages and secret rooms would be par for the course. Right?" Lexi reasoned.

"Lexi's idea really does make sense," Jennifer acknowledged. "Holly could have been spirited away easily."

"What about her coach, Tony?" Egg asked. "Wouldn't he have known something?"

"He wouldn't have to know where they took her. After all, he was blindfolded and gagged in the other passage," Lexi answered.

"I don't know if you're on the right track or not, Lexi, but it's worth a look." Todd motioned for her and Jennifer to jump in. "Come on. Let's drive past the house and see if that old blue car is still there."

They drove slowly up the street toward the Hanson mansion.

"It's gone!" Lexi gasped, her heart sinking. Had her wonderful idea been only wishful thinking? A dream that Holly would be found?

"There it is!" Binky pointed to the far end of the street. The old blue car was moving slowly toward them. It pulled onto a side street several yards from the front of the mansion. It looked like the driver didn't want to be connected with the old house in any way.

Todd pulled to the side of the road, jumped out of the car, threw open the hood and began to tinker with the engine.

"What are you doing?" Lexi whispered.

"Pretending I'm having car trouble. That way the guy won't think we're watching him."

After hesitating a few moments, the driver of the blue car seemed to realize the Ford Coupe wasn't going anywhere. Pulling his hat down low, he slipped out of his car and moved quickly toward the mansion, along the edge of the shrubs toward the back of the house and disappeared. As soon as he was gone, Todd slammed the hood on the Ford and jumped back into the car.

"Well, what did you see?"

"He got out of his car and went into the mansion," Lexi said, "but we couldn't see his face, he was too far away." Her heart was beating double time. "Now what do we do?"

Todd turned the key in the ignition and revved the motor. "We go to the police station."

———

"Ooooh, this is spooky," Binky announced as they walked up the steps to the police station.

"Everything is spooky to you, Binky," Egg pointed out.

"I've never been to a police station before. I don't think I like it."

"It's not so bad when you're going voluntarily,"

Todd said. "But I don't think I'd like it if I had to come here with a police escort. I wonder how the Hi-Fives felt when they came over here."

The group moved through the large double doors to the front desk. A uniformed policemen greeted them. "May I help you?"

"We'd like to talk to someone working on Holly Agnew's case," Todd said.

The policemen's eyebrows raised. "Oh you would, would you?"

"Yes. We have an idea of what may have happened to her and we'd like to talk to someone about it."

A smile pulled at the corners of his mouth. "Amateur detectives, I take it."

"You might call us that. Holly is a friend of ours. We've been trying to figure out this mystery, and we think we have it solved. Is there anyone here who could talk to us?" Lexi could tell the policemen was amused.

"Well, I imagine Detective Rose is the one you'd want to talk to. He's in the coffee room right now with one of the fellows from the FBI." The policeman pointed to his left. "Just go through that door and explain who you are."

Lexi could hear him chuckle as they moved toward the door. "Kids. What vivid imaginations they have."

The coffee room was bright and clean with a row of machines dispensing candy bars, hot chocolate and sandwiches. There were two men sitting at one of the long tables.

"Officer Rose?" Todd began.

One of the two men stood. He was a plainclothes-man dressed in a dark suit and a white shirt. The fact that he was a policeman was reinforced when he leaned over the table to shake Todd's hand and Lexi could see a shoulder holster strapped under his arm.

Todd introduced each of them. "Lexi has an idea about where Holly Agnew might be. We thought we should talk to you."

Detective Rose and the unintroduced FBI man turned to Lexi with questioning eyes. She felt a wave of nervous tension wash over her. This was very important, she realized. This was not kid stuff. She hoped they hadn't taken too much upon themselves.

Stammering slightly, she told them about the blue car. She talked about the secret passage and how there might be others. She mentioned the voices Holly insisted she'd heard the night before the tournament.

Todd added that they'd just driven by the house and the blue car had come back and a man had crept by way of the hedges to the back of the Hanson mansion. Both men were sitting straight up in their chairs now.

"You kids haven't made any of this up?" Detective Rose asked. "You're sure?"

Lexi's eyes grew wide and indignant. "Would we come here with a made-up story? This is very serious. Besides that—" and her voice quivered a little with emotion, "we don't lie."

Detective Rose looked apologetic. "I'm sorry. I didn't mean to insult you, but we may have to have someone check this out."

"Well, I should hope so," Egg sputtered. "Our

friend is kidnapped and we have a clue. You've *got* to check it out."

Detective Rose almost smiled. "I realize how involved you are, young man, but, several questions do arise. After all, Holly Agnew, her coach and entourage have come to us from out of town. Who could have imagined they would rent an entire house, or for that matter, that the house had secret passages—an ideal place to stage a kidnapping?"

"There are people in Cedar River who are familiar with the house," Jennifer offered.

"But did someone local rent it for them?" the officer asked. "Whoever did could be involved with the kidnappers."

Todd gave a sharp gasp of realization. "I know who rented the house. My own tennis coach. He works on the tournament committee."

Detective Rose looked at Todd intently. "Is that right?"

Todd nodded solemnly. "Holly's coach picked out the house himself. He didn't want the tennis committee involved. He had some very specific ideas about where he wanted to stay. My coach was in charge of doing the final paper work, but other than that, everything was taken care of through Holly's people."

Officer Rose glanced at the FBI man. "We'll have to talk to Tony Weare about this."

Todd nodded. "I remember Coach Barris saying to me, 'What an unusual name this man has—Anatoli H. Weare.'"

"What was that?" Officer Rose asked. What's his full name?"

"Anatoli H. Weare."

"What does the 'H' stand for?" Lexi wondered aloud.

Todd grew suddenly pale. "I never thought about it until now. Could it stand for Hanson?"

"You mean Holly's coach could be related to the family who owned the house?" Binky chattered excitedly.

"Yeah," Egg said, "and if he's related to the family who owned the house, he's probably been in the house before." He scratched his head, puzzled. "But if he'd been in the house before, why would he act like he hadn't known about the secret passages?"

The FBI agent swiftly rose to his feet. He placed his palms on the table and said evenly, "I'd like to thank you kids for coming to us with this information. We are going to search that house." Then he looked at Officer Rose. "In fact, why did we overlook that in the first place?"

"We did search the house, sir."

"What about the secret passages?"

"We followed the one that Weare was found in. It didn't seem to lead anywhere but the basement. I guess we just never suspected there'd be more than one."

"I'll bet it did lead to others," Lexi declared boldly. "If Holly heard voices in the walls, they could have come from anywhere in the house. There are probably other rooms closed off that no one has seen. That would explain why the house appears so huge from the outside, but once you get inside it doesn't seem all that big."

The FBI agent looked at Officer Rose. "We may

have to put these kids on the payroll."

"Can we watch?" Binky asked hopefully. "Can we be there when you search the house?"

Officer Rose shook his head. "Sorry kids. If there is something to this, we don't want to put you in any sort of danger."

Todd grabbed Egg by the arm. "Come on, let's get out of here. These guys have work to do."

Todd steered the group toward the car. "No one said we couldn't wait outside the Hanson mansion." They piled into the car and drove toward the house. All was quiet when they arrived. The blue car was still parked on the side street.

"It looks awfully dark and quiet," Binky said. "I'm not at all sure Holly's in there."

Lexi clutched her mid-section. "Oh, I'm so nervous. I'm so frightened for Holly. If I'm wrong, then this has been a wild goose chase and we still don't know where she is."

"When are her mom and dad coming?" Jennifer asked.

"Coach said they'd be here this morning," Todd answered. "They got the earliest flight they could."

"I feel sorry for them," Binky said sympathetically. "How terrible to hear that your daughter's been kidnapped."

Soon a stream of police cars came up the road. There were no sirens and no lights flashing. They pulled in quietly and several men stepped out.

"Are they going to stay in that house forever?" Binky asked, after thirty minutes had passed. "The house can't be *that* big or have that many secret passages."

As she spoke, a taxi pulled up in front of the mansion and a well-dressed middle-aged couple stepped out.

"Look! That must be Holly's parents," Jennifer pointed. "They're heading toward the house."

"Should we go talk to them?" Binky asked. "They look awfully upset."

Lexi put her hand on Binky's arm. "The police are inside. Maybe we should wait. We don't want to get into any trouble." As she spoke, the front door of the Hanson house flew open and two policemen stepped out. Behind them was Detective Rose, with a slight, unsteady figure with dark hair in tow.

"Holly!" Lexi gasped. "That's Holly!"

Pandemonium broke out in the car. "She *was* being kept in there! We were right. We were right! Can you believe it?" Squeals and hugs were exchanged all around.

"Ooooh, I want to get closer," Binky insisted. "I have to get out of the car."

"Wait, let Holly be with her parents," Lexi suggested. "We can talk to her later. There'll be plenty of time."

"Look!" Todd shouted. "It's Coach Weare." The dark and sullen man came out on the arms of two burly policemen. His hands were secured behind his back with handcuffs. His shoulders were slumped.

"Do you think he did it?" Egg asked. "Do you think he kidnapped Holly?"

"We'll just have to wait and see," Todd said calmly. "But it's not going to be long now."

The inside of the little old Ford reverberated with cheers.

Chapter Twelve

The tennis tournament was finally over. Holly Agnew was the undisputed champion. Every performance was magnificent. Though she'd been sheltered and protected diligently by her parents ever since the kidnapping incident, they had agreed to allow Holly to come to the celebration party at Lexi's home. Egg, Binky, Todd, Jennifer and Lexi were all pacing nervously back and forth in front of the door waiting for their guest of honor.

"I hope she comes early so we can talk to her in private," Binky fumed. "I want to hear what's been going on."

"Her parents have certainly been staying close since this incident," Jennifer commented.

"Wouldn't you if your child had been kidnapped?" Egg asked.

"I suppose, but I think I'd let her see her friends."

"Here she comes now," Lexi said eagerly.

Holly stepped out of the car and waved to her father. By the time she reached the front step, all five of her friends were waiting on the porch. Lexi flung her arms around Holly. "I am so glad you are all right. We were so frightened for you."

"I was scared, too," Holly said. "And I heard through Detective Rose that I have you guys to thank for my rescue."

Lexi blushed. "No, not really. They would have found you anyway."

"But it might have taken them much longer. Very clever of you. The police never thought of looking for more secret passages in the house." Holly shuddered. "I'm so glad they did. It was horrible in that dark, dusty place."

Jennifer took Holly by the hand and pulled her into the house. "Come inside and tell us all about it. Why did he do it? Why did your coach kidnap you?"

Holly's face crumpled. Lexi was afraid her friend might cry. "This is the biggest disappointment of my life," she said. "I trusted Coach Weare. And look what he did to me! It seems the only reason he ever coached me was because he wanted my father's money. He knew he was good enough to coach any of a number of rising tennis stars, but he picked me. He knew about my father's wealth and saw a way to get his hands on some of it.

"Coach Weare had been working for months to get into my family's good graces so they would allow him to bring me to Cedar River without them. Usually my parents travel with me, but since Coach Weare had been so charming and persuasive, they decided that I could go alone. My dad also remembered that Tony had once said he had a distant relative in Cedar River. I suppose Dad thought a contact would help, that Coach Weare would have someone he knew to stay with, and I'd have a homecooked meal or two. What he didn't mention to father was that he'd spent several summers in the Hanson mansion as a child and knew all the secret passages and hidden doors."

"You mean he was acquainted with everything in the house before he came?" Binky asked.

"Tony's mother's maiden name was Hanson. When he was a little boy they visited here. That was before Peter Hanson's fiancee was murdered by a prowler, of course. Tony scouted the house out as a boy, and knew how to get into all the secret passages. Do you know that the inside of that house is a virtual maze of secret hallways and small rooms?"

"What were they used for?" Lexi asked.

"Who knows? Apparently the whole family was eccentric. They were always taking precautions against what they called the 'outside world.' I don't know if they expected to be attacked or robbed, or thought that someday they'd need a place to hide. The whole house is like a honeycomb. Anyway, Tony had spent so much time in that weird house he knew how to get from the first floor to the third without ever being seen, and how to listen to conversations from behind walls.

"The night I couldn't sleep, he was talking to one of the men he insisted travel with us on this trip. Apparently they were all in it together and had planned to split the ransom money—even the bodyguard and my tutor! What Tony didn't realize was that the voices sometimes carried from one part of the house to another. They weren't anywhere near my room; yet, when they conversed, the sounds carried through the walls. Unfortunately, I couldn't hear well enough to decipher what they were saying or all of this might have been prevented."

"He'd planned to do this all along?" Binky was indignant.

"We don't know how long ago Tony devised the scheme to kidnap me, but as soon as he decided, he knew he would keep me in the house. He knew how difficult it was to get into the secret passages and that it would be sheer luck on the part of the police if they found their way into one. Besides that, the passages, though connected, have false walls between them. You need to know the secret of getting from one part of the house to another."

"I'm still confused," Binky said. "If he was the one who kidnapped you, how come they found him tied up in that first passage?"

"Oh, he'd planned that, too. That was to divert any suspicion away from himself. He had one of his own men tie him up and plant the note. That's why Tony wasn't hurt any worse by the so-called intruder. Then his men left the house and spent the day at the tennis courts. No one would ever suspect my coach, he decided, especially if he'd been tied up."

"Why did he use the secret passage for himself?"

"I suppose he knew that there were rumors around town that the house might have one, and the logical spot would be off my bedroom since it's the one old man Hanson stayed in himself. Tony was probably pretty certain no one would suspect more than one passage. He had an accomplice hiding with me in one of the secret rooms. I was bound and gagged so I couldn't make any noise. The accomplices had been staying in the house since before Tony and I arrived."

"He thought of everything, didn't he?" Egg's voice held a feeling of awe.

"Not everything. Tony was smart, but his accomplices weren't smart enough to move the old car."

"So they *are* the owners of the blue car."

Holly nodded. "They were the ones that followed me around everywhere. That car was Lexi's clue to my being found. Lexi, I think you're the smartest girl in the whole country right now," Holly said with genuine appreciation. "If it hadn't been for you, I don't know what might have happened to me."

"I've always thought she was the smartest girl around," Todd said proudly.

"Me too," chimed Egg and Binky.

Jennifer laughed. "I might think that too, but I'm not telling her. I don't want her to get a big head. She's too good a friend for that."

"Thanks a lot, Jennifer," Lexi said.

Just then the doorbell rang and the rest of the partygoers arrived. It was several hours later before Holly was able to be alone again with her friends. She stood at the doorway, her eyes brimming with tears. "You guys are the greatest. I'm so glad I got to meet you all while I was here in Cedar River."

"You're the celebrity, Holly," Lexi asserted, "and you're the one that's terrific."

They all exchanged addresses, hugs and promises to write. Binky gave a loud sniffle as Holly departed. "I hate saying good-bye," she said. She rubbed at her eyes with a fist. "It's so depressing."

"Well, Holly's not leaving forever," Lexi assured her. "She said she'd come back to visit when she could. And she did promise to write."

"We'll all be old ladies before she gets back," Binky predicted mournfully. "I just know it."

"Binky, even when you're a hundred and five you still won't be an old lady," Todd said with a laugh. "Besides that, my tennis coach said that the tournament was such a success that they're planning on having another one in two years. They've already begun the arrangements."

"That means Holly will be back?"

"We hope so."

"By that time, she might be such a big name she won't bother with a place as insignificant as Cedar River," Egg said. "But after all that's happened to her here, you never know."

————

"Anybody home?" Jennifer called. She stuck her head inside the screen door of the Leighton home. "Lexi, are you in there?"

"Coming. I'm just getting my swimsuit."

"Hurry up. Egg and Binky left a half hour ago and I know Todd's already there."

"It'll feel so good to swim again," Lexi said as she trotted down the stairs in a hot pink jumper she'd made herself. "It's been a crazy summer already, hasn't it?"

"Crazy, but fun. I feel sorry for Peggy, Anna Marie and Matt. They've missed out on all the excitement."

"I wouldn't have minded missing out on *some* of the excitement," Lexi said. She shuddered a little. "Especially the part about the kidnapping."

"Well, we can forget about that now. Let's just go

to the pool and soak up some rays."

The girls rode their bikes to the public pool. As they approached the gate they could hear happy shouts and splashing. Lexi spotted Todd and Binky stretched out on beach blankets on the far side.

"Where's Egg?" she wondered aloud.

Jennifer glanced around. "Who knows with him . . . Oh, there he is. Tiptoeing around so he won't be detected."

"By whom?"

"I don't know. He's over by the Hi-Fives now. He claims they treat him like he's invisible. So I guess he's acting like he is."

"He's up to something, Jennifer. I can tell. He's acting very odd."

Egg crept between the sunning girls looking like a gawking flamingo with his long, scrawny build.

"Let's go see what he's up to." Jennifer led the way. "All the Hi-Fives are here. Let's see if any of them will speak to us after their humbling trip to the police station and park board."

"You're a glutton for punishment," Lexi said with a laugh. "I don't think one confession will keep them humble for long." As the girls walked past, none of the Hi-Fives, including Minda Hannaford and Tressa Williams, raised their heads. Bottles of suntan oil and lotion were scattered everywhere.

Jennifer and Lexi reached Binky and Todd. "Hi, what's Egg up to?"

"Oh, who knows?" Binky said disgustedly. "He's off on some sort of a mission. He's acting really strange today. Secretive. Like he has something up his sleeve. As soon as we got here, he went tiptoeing over to where the Hi-Fives are. I'm ignoring him. My brother is just too bizarre for words."

Todd patted the concrete next to him. "Put your towel here, Lexi."

It took Lexi a few minutes to settle herself and apply her suntan lotion. Then she leaned back, closed her eyes and allowed the sun's warming rays to soak into her body.

"Oh, this feels wonderful," she sighed. "I didn't realize how tense I was over Holly until just now. I finally feel my body relaxing." She opened one eye and looked at Todd. "Do you know what time it is? I don't want to burn."

"It's two-thirty," he said. "If you're worried about anyone getting burned, you should talk to the Hi-Fives. They've been laying there like blocks of wood for over an hour without moving."

"Tell me about it," Jennifer snorted. "They didn't even open an eyelid when we walked by."

It was nearly three o'clock when Lexi sat up and stretched. "I think I'd better put on some real sunblock," she announced to no one in particular. "I don't want to get fried."

"Looks like the Hi-Fives just had the same thought," Todd observed.

Minda was oiling herself while Tressa Williams squirted lotion on her sister's back. "Do you notice how they do everything together, even to putting on suntan lotion?" Binky commented sarcastically. "I'm so glad I'm not part of that group. It's like they tell each other when to breathe."

Suddenly, the air was filled with shrieks and screams. "No, oh no!"

"What's happening?"

"Oh, gross!"

"What's going on over there?" Jennifer sat up and peered in the direction of the commotion.

Several of Minda's friends were standing up now, squealing, screaming, and trying in vain to wipe off the streaks of red, blue and green from their bodies.

"What did they put on themselves? They look like rainbows!" Binky squealed.

"I've got blue stuff all over my legs," Minda shrieked. "And green—and red. Oh, ick. This is so gross!"

The girls carried on until a lifeguard strolled over to check out the situation. "All right, girls. I don't know what the problem is, but you'd better calm down or move out. You're disturbing everyone else here," he said sternly.

"We aren't up to anything," Minda protested. "Look at us. We're covered with this . . . stuff. We don't know where it came from."

The lifeguard's eyes narrowed. "Whatever it is, you'd better not enter the water with it. We just cleaned the pool and we can't have any contamination in it."

"You're kicking us out of the *public* pool?" Minda was indignant.

"We can't have unnecessary disturbance, Miss. And we can't allow you into the pool with something other than suntan lotion. Come back tomorrow."

Minda's face flushed pink. She bent to gather her towel and lotions. "I'm going to tell my father about this. You can't kick us out of here. This is an insult."

The lifeguard stood firm, his muscular arms

crossed over his chest. "I can send anybody out of here that's causing a disturbance." He eyed Minda's streaked arms and legs with an annoyed look.

Just then, Egg came tiptoeing up and sank down on a towel next to Binky. "Where have you been?" she asked suspiciously.

"And what did you have to do with the High-Fives?" Todd demanded to know.

Egg looked innocent and surprised at Todd's accusation. Then the corners of his mouth turned upward and he began to smile. Quickly the smile turned into an outright laugh. "I just gave them a taste of their own medicine, that's all. They think they're so smart pulling pranks and laughing when other people are upset. I think they got off too easy just having to confess what they did. I thought it would be good for them to know what it felt like."

"Egg McNaughton, what did you do?" Binky demanded.

Egg opened his hands to reveal an eyedropper and several small bottles of food coloring. "I just put a drop or two in each of their bottles of suntan lotion. I thought they should get a taste of how hard it is to remove food coloring. After all, city maintenance had to clean it out of the fountains all over town."

"You put food coloring in their suntan lotion?" Binky gasped, covering her mouth with her hand.

Just then, Minda stalked by the small group, her arms and legs streaked red and blue. She stopped in front of them and glared accusingly at Egg. "You had something to do with this, Egg McNaughton. I saw you tiptoeing around us—I should have known you were up to something."

"Why, Minda, I can't understand why *you'd* be upset with anyone," Egg said innocently. "After all, *you're* the one who likes to play pranks. *You're* the one who thinks they're funny. In fact, wasn't it *you* who said this town was boring? Well, I just wanted to liven it up a bit!"

Minda's face turned bright red. "Egg Mc-Naughton, you are the most infuriating boy I've ever met." With that, she gave a small huff and stomped off.

Egg grinned at her receding figure. Slowly, casually, he placed his hands behind his head and lay down on his towel. With a blissful sigh, he closed his eyes. "Well, what do you know, gang, I finally got Minda Hannaford to notice me!"

———

Will Peggy and Chad's problems ever end? Even though Peggy is pulling her life together, Chad's seems to be falling apart. Read about it in Cedar River Daydreams Number 13, *No Turning Back.*

A Note From Judy

I'm glad you're reading *Cedar River Daydreams*!
I hope I've given you something to think about as
well as a story to entertain you. If you feel you have
any of the problems that Lexi and her friends experience, I encourage you to talk with your parents, a
pastor, or a trusted adult friend. There are many people who care about you!

Also, I enjoy hearing from my readers, so if you'd
like to write, my address is:

> Judy Baer
> Bethany House Publishers
> 6820 Auto Club Road
> Minneapolis, MN 55438

*Please include an <u>addressed, stamped envelope</u> if
you would like an answer. Thanks.*